ALSO BY CAROL HIGGINS CLARK

CAROL
HIGGINS CLARK

JINXED

A Regan Reilly Mystery

SCRIBNER

New York London Toronto Sydney Singapore

F

SCRIBNER
1230 Avenue of the Americas
New York, NY 10020

Copyright © 2002 by Carol Higgins Clark
All rights reserved, including the right of
reproduction in whole or in part in any form.

SCRIBNER and design are trademarks of
Macmillan Library Reference USA, Inc., used under license
by Simon & Schuster, the publisher of this work.

For information regarding special discounts for bulk purchases,
please contact Simon & Schuster Special Sales at
1-800-456-6798 or business@simonandschuster.com

Designed by Kyoko Watanabe
Text set in Baskerville

Manufactured in the United States of America

1   3   5   7   9   10   8   6   4   2

Library of Congress Cataloging-in-Publication Data is available.

ISBN 0-7432-0582-0

Acknowledgments

I would like to thank the following people who were so helpful to me as I wrote this book.

First and foremost, my editor, Roz Lippel, who is such a pleasure to work with and a great adviser and sounding board. Roz's assistant, Laura Petermann, was ever helpful. Special thanks to Michael Korda and Chuck Adams for their guidance. A cheer for my publicist, Lisl Cade, who, as always, is right there for me. Thanks to my agent, Nick Ellison, and my foreign rights director, Alicka Pistek.

Art director John Fulbrook has once again done a terrific job as has associate director of copyediting Gypsy da Silva. Also, a special nod to the memory of copyeditor Carol Catt. And as always thanks, Mom! My mother, Mary Higgins Clark, is always at the other end of the phone when I need encouragement!

Finally, thanks to my family and friends who are always asking, "How's it going?"

Now I can play!

In memory of my grandmothers,
Nora Cecelia Higgins and Alma Claire Clark,
with joy and love!

Thursday, May 9

1

———◆———

"Turn right at the bumpy dirt road," Regan Reilly instructed her beau, Jack "no relation" Reilly. He was at the wheel of her Lexus, and they were heading to the last winery on their tour of the Napa Valley and Santa Barbara County. Regan was reading from a guidebook.

"This bumpy dirt road?" Jack asked as he made the turn and the car started to bounce along, stirring up a cloud of dust in its wake.

Regan smiled. "I don't see any others."

"I can just imagine what this place is going to be like," Jack mused. "With a name like 'Altered States' and this out-of-the-way location . . ."

"They say it's the perfect place to relax, sip a glass of wine, meditate, sleep in the charming bed-and-breakfast . . . get away from it all, and leave your stress behind."

"Well, they were right when they said we were getting away from it all." Jack reached over and squeezed Regan's hand. "This place is way off the beaten track. And in the last week we've been to some remote spots."

Regan and Jack had met five months ago in New York when Regan's father, Luke, was kidnapped at Christmastime. Jack, the head of the Major Case Squad in Manhattan, had been instrumental in finding Luke.

Luke was returned safely on Christmas Eve. Regan and Jack's romance began that night. Perhaps an odd way for two people to meet, yet Luke claimed full credit and protested that he had not yet been paid his Dolly Levi commission. He and Regan's mother, suspense writer Nora Regan Reilly, were convinced that Jack was Regan's perfect match. Not only was thirty-four-year-old Jack handsome, nice, and smart, with a wry sense of humor, but he also was a go-getter. A graduate of Boston College, he had two master's degrees, and his goal was to become police commissioner of New York. Few who knew him doubted he would make it.

Now they were finishing up their first vacation together, a driving tour that took them north from Los Angeles, up the Pacific Coast Highway, and across to the Napa Valley wine country, then back down through the valleys. Altered States was their last stop before heading back to Los Angeles where thirty-one-year-old Regan worked as a private investigator.

The trip had been great. They'd walked the beach, stopped in little coastal towns, and discovered restaurants that were full of charm and good food. Even the characters in a couple of roadside dumps they'd stumbled upon provided a lot of laughs.

"You know," Jack said, smiling, "we haven't gotten on each other's nerves even once."

"What a miracle." Regan laughed as she glanced at his profile. God, is he good-looking, she thought. And he makes me so happy. He was 6 feet 2 inches tall, broad-shouldered, with sandy brown hair that tended to curl, strong even features, and hazel eyes. He was the perfect complement to Regan, who had inherited Black Irish looks from the Reilly side of her family. She had raven black hair, light skin, and blue eyes.

"This is the bumpy dirt road to end all bumpy dirt roads." Jack navigated the car down the seemingly endless stretch. It was almost five o'clock. They had been driving for hours and were looking forward to getting out of the car and having a glass of wine on the back deck of the inn that supposedly had a great panoramic view.

In the distance, they saw a cluster of old wooden and stone buildings, surrounded by acres and acres of vineyards. Regan whispered, "It does have the feeling of an old ghost town, just as the guidebook promised."

"This place was abandoned for decades, right?" Jack asked.

"Yes. Prohibition put the winery out of business, and then it stood idle for years. A couple bought it and started renovations, but then they went bankrupt. The new owners haven't had it for long at all."

They drove slowly through a lemon grove and into the open space in front of the main building. Jack stopped the car. They got out, and each took a deep breath of the fragrant air.

"It's so peaceful and quiet," Regan said.

Jack's cell phone rang. "You were saying," he remarked as he winked at her, pulled open his phone, and answered it. Regan could tell right away from the tone of his voice that it was his office calling. She slowly walked over to the large stone building and stepped inside the main entrance.

"Hello there." A tall, thin woman greeted Regan quietly from behind a massive reception desk. Numerous candles flickered on a shelf behind the desk. The woman looked about fifty and had flowing blond hair streaked with gray that gave her an ethereal quality. "We're so glad to have you here at Altered States."

This certainly feels like Altered States, Regan thought, but she said, "Thank you. It's nice to be here."

"Do you have a reservation?"

"Yes, we do."

"Wonderful. Please sign our guest book. Where are you from?"

"Los Angeles."

"That's great. Do you have a business card? We'd like to make sure you're on our mailing list."

Regan pulled a card from her wallet and handed it to the woman.

The woman stared at it for a moment, then looked up at Regan with a Zen-like expression. "You're a private investigator?"

Regan nodded. "Yes."

"How neat," she said. "That is really neat."

"Oh, it's neat all right," Regan agreed and laughed. She could hear the door behind her open. She turned, already smiling, praying it would be Jack. This woman was just a little odd. Her prayers were answered, but Jack was not looking as relaxed as he had a few minutes before.

"I'm sorry, Regan. I have to get back to New York tomorrow. That case I told you about . . ."

Regan felt a stab of acute disappointment. "Oh, Jack, that means our vacation's over," she said with a look of mock horror.

"I know. I feel terrible. We should probably go down to Los Angeles tonight."

The woman behind the desk looked sympathetic. "We'll be happy to honor your reservation another time. We'd just love to have you come back and visit."

"We'd love to come back," Jack and Regan replied in unison, as a black cat jumped up on the desk.

None of them had any clue that Regan would be returning in less than twenty-four hours.

2

———◆———

Lucretia Standish pushed the "help" button on her night table for the third time since she'd awakened in her sumptuous bedroom in Beverly Hills. She hadn't lived in the house long and still got a kick out of pushing the button vigorously every time a thought crossed her mind that might require feedback from the maid. The maid, making a concerted effort not to go mad, longed for her old employer, who died as she had lived, peacefully, only three months before. The house had been sold, furniture included, to Lucretia.

Lucretia was ninety-three years old and had no time to waste on decorating. "It takes years to get it right. You put something on order, and it takes forever. I haven't got forever. I like this place as is. I want to buy the whole kit and caboodle."

"But the family might not want—" the real estate agent had protested.

"I'm making an offer. Take it or leave it."

The next of kin were only too happy not to have to deal with a full-blown garage sale.

The house was perfect for Lucretia. It was elegant yet comfortable, a ranch with a large garden and pool. Everything in the bedroom, from the plush carpeting to the silk curtains to the fluffy quilt and dozens of decorative pillows, was done in shades of peach—tones and textures that were designed to soothe. A big job for these inanimate objects; some might say impossible. Lucretia could be a handful.

She had done a lot of living in her ninety-three years. Her father had owned a winery that went out of business, thanks to Prohibition. When she was a teenager, Lucretia moved to Hollywood where she became a promising young actress in silent films. She was just starting to get famous when they began making talkies. Lo and behold, Lucretia's screechy voice killed any hope of a transition. Then the stock market crashed on her birthday.

"Timing is everything," Lucretia would say. "And mine often stinks. The 1920s were not so roaring for my family." Then, with a mischievous smile, she'd always add, "But the last seventy years haven't been bad." Her optimism about life never flagged.

Lucretia had married five times, traveled around the world, and lived on three continents. When her last husband, Haskell Weldon, died while playing bingo on a world cruise, Lucretia returned to their apartment in New York City. A young man she met at a party told her he had a hot investment tip.

"There's a new dot-com that's going to go through the roof," he whispered. "If I were you, I'd invest every penny I could spare."

"What's a dot-com?" she asked.

Thirteen glorious months later, believing that nothing good lasts forever, Lucretia cashed out, just before the company went belly-up. With nearly $60 million in her bank account, she decided to sell the New York apartment and move back to California where the weather was better. Driving around Beverly Hills on her first Sunday back, she noticed that the house she had always admired when she was a young actress with stars in her eyes had a FOR SALE sign in front of it—OPEN HOUSE TODAY.

"It's meant to be," she cried, jumping out of the car and running inside. Lucretia wasted no time in making an offer.

"I had my heart set on this place over seventy years ago. I might be a little old to have the wild parties I would have had if things had worked out back then, but now I'm living my dream!" she explained to the real estate agent. Two weeks later the house was hers.

Lucretia pushed the button again, and the maid hurried into the room. "Yes, Miss Lucretia."

"Phyllis, why isn't Edward here yet?" Lucretia asked a trifle impatiently. Although Lucretia's voice had stopped her acting career dead in its tracks, at ninety-three she still sounded surprisingly strong and snappy. She was a tiny little thing with wispy strawberry-colored hair and delicate features. Her skin was creamy and taut, thanks to genetics and an occasional nip and tuck. It was easy to see why the camera had loved her. Too bad the same couldn't be said about the microphone. There was no romance there. It only brought out the worst in her.

"Beats me." Phyllis, a woman in her early sixties, did not waste words. Her passion was game shows, and she had appeared as a contestant on several over the years. She was a stocky woman with a bulldog face and drooping lower lip that gave her a mournful expression.

Lucretia shrugged. "Me, too." She knew it was a silly question. Edward wasn't due for another ten minutes. "I'll go sit at the table on the patio. Send him out there as soon as he arrives."

"Of course." Phyllis hurried back to the kitchen where, on the miniature television set on the counter, a contestant was about to play for big money.

Eight minutes later, Edward Fields pulled up the driveway in his BMW. Lucretia had phoned him very early and said she needed to talk. She had made a lot of money thanks to Edward's hot tip, and she trusted him. That was good, he thought. He needed her. He was now managing her money, and she was his only game in town. He had followed her from New York to California.

Forty-six years old, he had a carefully cultivated nerdy appearance. Three old ladies ago, he realized that what worked best was to look like a cross between a benevolent church usher and a scrupulous accountant, someone who cared about your welfare and your bank account. Short, gelled brown hair parted in a razor-sharp line and a perpetually earnest expression emanating from sad brown eyes behind horn-rimmed glasses did the trick.

Edward parked the car, pulled his briefcase off the seat next to him, and opened the door. His thin frame was clothed in a conservative gray suit. A white shirt and black bow tie completed the outfit.

"She's out back," Phyllis announced curtly when she answered the door, nodding toward the pool.

"Thank you, ma'am," Edward replied with exaggerated politeness. He hated to admit that he was a little afraid of her. She had Lucretia's ear when he wasn't around, and he had the feeling that she saw through him. Kill the enemy with kindness, he thought every time he laid eyes on her bulldog face.

He found Lucretia at a table by the swimming pool. Clad in a multicolored caftan, she was sitting under a pink umbrella sipping pink lemonade.

"Darling!" she cried when she saw him.

"Lucretia." He leaned down to kiss her cheek, stood up, and looked around. "I can't get over how much I love it back here. This is so perfect for you. I'm so glad you were able to finally own this house."

What he was trying to get to run through her mind once

again was that it was all thanks to him. He did this as often as possible, walking a fine line between subtlety and hitting her over the head.

"I love it, too," Lucretia said excitedly as she admired the glistening water sprinkled with floating striped beach balls, the lush manicured yard, and the little pool house painted a perky pink to match the umbrella. "And I've decided it's time I had a party."

"That's a great idea!" Edward said, thinking of who he would invite. Who he needed to impress.

"A family party," Lucretia added. "That's what I wanted to talk to you about today."

"Family party?" Edward looked surprised. He'd never met any of her family. He didn't think she had any living relatives. For some reason he was starting to sweat.

"My dear Haskell had a niece, two nephews, and one grand-niece. They all live in California. I want to connect with them."

The children of her late husband's brother were "hippie types," she explained. They all looked for an inner peace that didn't come from soothing peach bed pillows. Just before Haskell died, they purchased an old ghost winery. It had been abandoned for years after Prohibition. The previous owners had gone bankrupt, and the three siblings bought it for a song. Their plan was to add a meditation center, a spa, and a candle shop. They had called Haskell for advice, and he told them to go for it. "Think big," he preached. "That's why I was a success."

They hadn't been too happy when their uncle told them two years earlier that he was marrying Lucretia. He'd known her so briefly. Lucretia and Haskell married in Europe, lived in New York, and spent most of their two-year union on cruise ships, so Lucretia had never met Haskell's family. A get-together was just being planned when a strenuous game of bingo did him in.

"Why do you want to connect with them?" Edward asked, his voice almost squeaking. God, he thought, I don't need family members getting in the way.

"Because I want them to be at our wedding," Lucretia answered, smiling up at him. "I've decided to accept your proposal."

Edward grabbed Lucretia's fragile little hand and brought it to his lips. "My love," he whispered. "I'm overwhelmed. I never thought you would—"

"I didn't, either," Lucretia admitted. "But you've been so wonderful to me. I must say that when I was younger, you wouldn't have been my type. Quite frankly, I preferred men who were dashing and exciting. But now that I'm more mature, I realize how important it is to have someone who is serious and caring and concerned—"

"I am those and more," he managed to croak, slightly insulted yet glad that his act had gone over so well. "Why don't we just elope today?"

Lucretia laughed. "You bad boy! I want to make amends with Haskell's family. I want them at the wedding. They never accepted me because they thought I wanted their uncle's money. But that wasn't it at all. Haskell and I loved each other. I've decided that I'm going to take the original eight million dollars he left me and give it to them. Two million each. It will be a surprise. The rest is ours!"

"More lemonade?"

Lucretia and Edward both turned to see Phyllis standing there with a pitcher in hand.

"Not now, Phyllis!" Lucretia snapped.

Phyllis beat a quick retreat back to the kitchen.

Edward's head was spinning. Give away eight million, he thought glumly for about a nanosecond. But then he thought of all those other millions that would someday be his alone . . .

Lucretia wrapped her hands around his. "You have your homes in the south of France and New York. I have this wonderful dreamhouse. We can live here. I don't want to travel anymore, though. A fortune-teller once told me that I was going to die abroad. So I figure from now on, I'll just stay home! I hope you don't mind . . ."

"Not at all," he answered almost too quickly.

She patted the seat next to her. "Sit down, darling. We'll plan the wedding for this Sunday."

"Sunday?" Edward gasped.

"Four days from now. I can hardly wait. I was up all night thinking about the celebration we'll have. I couldn't sleep, so I dug out the photo album that Haskell's niece and nephews gave him just before we met. I must ask Phyllis to start calling them immediately and give them the good news so they can make plans to be here Sunday."

Edward pulled out his handkerchief and wiped the sweat that had trickled down from the base of his perfectly parted hair. His palms felt clammy. On Sunday he would be worth $52 million.

Lucretia opened the photo album. "I want us both to recognize everyone and remember their names. We'll all be one big happy family. It would make dear Haskell so happy." Lucretia pointed at a picture of a middle-aged guy with a shaved head who looked as if he were wearing a pair of pajamas. "Now this is Earl. He is the one who loves to meditate, the poor dear. And this is Leon. He's the one who runs the winery." Lucretia shrugged. "I think of my poor father. He had a wonderful winery, and then the government decided that drinking was a sin." She turned the page. "Here is Lilac with all her candles and incense. Stuff makes me itch." She turned and looked at Edward. He was staring at the picture below Lilac's. "What's the matter, dear?"

Edward pointed to the picture of an attractive blond in her mid-twenties.

"Who's that?" He coughed, trying to conceal the fear in his voice.

"That's Lilac's daughter. Her name is Freshness."

"Freshness?" Edward repeated, suddenly relieved.

Lucretia rolled her eyes. "That's what her mother named her when she was born. Something about the air being so fresh that day. A hippie name. But even Freshness knew it sounded ridiculous, so when she became an actress, she decided to use the name Whitney. Whitney Weldon. Apparently she's gotten some nice little parts in movies."

Edward felt the blood drain from his head. "You're inviting her to the wedding?"

"Of course. I'm dying to talk to her about acting. I still miss it! She's the one I really want to spend time with on Sunday."

Not if I can help it, Edward thought as he tried to remain calm. I will prevent it, he promised himself. There was no way he was going to let Freshness ruin his wedding day.

No matter what it took.

Friday, May 10

3

————◆————

Regan unlocked the door to her office and stepped over the pile of mail that had accumulated on the floor. She felt as if it had already been a long day, and it was only 8:00 A.M. She'd dropped Jack off at the airport at seven and decided to come in to work to catch up on things.

Normally, Regan loved working. But not today. Even though Regan's body had made it to the office, her mind was someplace else: still on vacation with Jack. But he was gone, and she wouldn't see him for another two weeks, when she'd fly back to New York for Memorial Day weekend.

Willing herself to be productive, she put the brown bag containing a cup of coffee and a blueberry muffin on her desk, let her purse slide down off her arm, and bent down to pick up the mail. Straightening up, she glanced around the familiar surroundings. Usually her home away from home was a great comfort, but today it had a lonesome, almost neglected feeling. Like me, she thought.

The office was in an old building near Hollywood and Vine that had black-and-white tile floors, ancient plumbing in the bathroom, and, some say, ghosts in the hallways. It felt just right to Regan. No sleek new office building for her. She preferred character in a joint.

Regan walked over to the casement window and pushed it open. A cool morning breeze filtered in. "That's good," Regan mumbled to herself. "Get this place aired out. Time to get moving."

Flipping the lid off her coffee cup, she sat down in the chair that had promised to give everything from back support to unconditional love, and had cost her a fortune. She took a sip of the coffee and started sorting through what was a lot of junk mail when the phone rang, piercing the quiet.

A look of puzzlement crossed Regan's face as she mentally reviewed who could possibly be calling this early. Her mother was in Los Angeles on a book tour. Her father had flown in yesterday to spend a few days with Nora and meet with producers about a film adaptation of her latest book. Jack and Regan had a late dinner with them last night. They wouldn't be calling this early. And Jack should be somewhere over the state of Nevada by now.

The phone rang again. Probably a sales call, Regan thought as she grabbed the receiver. "Regan Reilly."

"Is this Regan herself?" a breathy woman's voice asked.

"It is."

"I'm so glad you're there. Hi."

"Well, hi. How can I help you?"

The caller sighed. "Oh, this whole thing is so weird. Okay. Now. Let's see. . . ."

Regan picked up a pen and pulled a legal pad closer to her as she waited for the caller to say something worth writing down. The woman sounded like a space cadet. But the call helped Regan get her mind off the fact that she wished she were still on vacation with Jack.

"Actually, we sort of met yesterday—at Altered States."

Regan's eyebrows raised. "Oh, you were the woman at the desk."

"Yes, that's right. My name is Lilac Weldon. I'm so glad I found out you were a private investigator. I think it was Kismet."

"Kismet?" Regan repeated. "Why was it Kismet?"

Lilac cleared her throat gently and lowered her voice. "Yesterday I heard from the maid of an elderly actress my uncle married a few years back. He's dead now, and she is getting remarried. She wants my two brothers and my daughter and me to come to the wedding this Sunday."

So far, so good, Regan thought.

"The thing is, we haven't been close at all. We've never even met this woman. They were married only a couple of years, and he left everything to her. We didn't get a dime. Not even a nickel. Not one single penny. Anyway, I was polite and said it was awfully short notice, that I'd have to see. Maybe we could visit another time—ya know, blah blah blah. This Sunday is Mother's Day, and we're busy. I guess the maid could tell I had no intention of coming."

Regan still hadn't written anything down.

"So the maid calls me back early this morning. You could have knocked me over with a feather. She told me that she thought Lucretia—that's who's getting married—was planning to give us the money our uncle had left her if we came to the wedding. But she wasn't going to tell us about it. She wanted to see if we'd bother to show up. If we *all* showed up, she'd fork it over."

"How much?" Regan asked.

"Two million each."

"I'll go," Regan offered.

Lilac laughed nervously. "Oh, I know. It's kind of crazy. But Lucretia made over $50 million off a dot-com. Well, I just talked to my brothers, and they want to go to the wedding."

Naturally, Regan thought.

"I mean we could use the money. We sunk all our money into this place when we bought it, and it still needs a lot of work. But the thing is, my daughter is gone until Sunday night. She's going to come here for dinner for Mother's Day, which will be too late."

"You can't call her?"

"Well, she's an actress and lives in Los Angeles, but she has a part in a movie that's filming near Santa Barbara. I talked to her yesterday morning before I heard about the wedding, and she said she had off Friday and wasn't sure what she was doing for the next few days. It's one of her go-with-the-flow weekends."

"Go-with-the-flow weekends?"

"Sometimes she just likes to get in her car and take off and be alone and out of touch for a couple of days. Be out of touch so she can get in touch with her inner self. Commune with nature, you know? I tried her hotel room this morning, and there's no answer. I left a message, but she may be gone already."

"Doesn't she have a cell phone?" Regan asked.

"Cell phones are a no-no on go-with-the-flow weekends. She has it with her but only uses it for emergencies, like if her car breaks down. Otherwise, she says it stresses her out to be constantly checking messages and answering the phone. So for all intents and purposes she has probably disappeared until dinnertime on Sunday."

That would be a drag, Regan thought. It amazed her that someone could take off like that and be unreachable. Being Irish, she was always expecting the other shoe to drop. It would make her too anxious to think that her parents couldn't get hold of her. But these people were of a different mind-set. "What is your daughter's name?" she asked.

"Freshness."

"Freshness?"

"Yes. Freshness. She was born on the most glorious spring morning. But now she goes by Whitney."

Score one for the daughter, Regan mused. "Lilac, what would you like me to do?"

"Find Freshness." She paused. "Regan, we all could really use the money. We have debts and—"

"I understand," Regan said quickly. Then suddenly she wondered why the maid bothered to contact Lilac about the money. Could it be some sort of ruse? "You know, you might not be getting any money at all," Regan cautioned. "Who knows whether the maid was telling you the truth?"

"I thought of that," Lilac said. "But on the chance that it's on the level, it certainly won't hurt us to make the trip. Uncle Haskell was a good guy, and he must have liked this lady. It still hurt that he didn't leave us anything. The other thing is . . ." Her voice broke. "Regan, all of a sudden I'm worried about Freshness. I can't explain it . . . but I have the feeling that something bad is going to happen to her if you don't find her before Sunday. Did you ever get a feeling like that?"

"Oh, yes," Regan said quietly. "And my superstitious Irish grandmother had premonitions all the time, and they often came true. Now let's start with some facts. Where is the movie being filmed? I can drive up there and talk to people on the set. And what's the name of the movie?"

Lilac hesitated before she answered Regan's last question. "The movie is *Jinxed*."

4

Eddie Fields hadn't slept a wink all night. He had the brass ring just within his grasp, and now one little jerk named Freshness could ruin everything. Why did he ever take that acting class in New York anyway? He thought it would help him perfect his role as a conservative investment adviser, but he didn't need any help at that. He was a master at deceiving people.

Whitney Weldon was in that class. They were to do a scene together, so they rehearsed at his apartment. A friend of his had called and left a message on the answering machine while they were going over their lines. Eddie hadn't thought to turn the volume down.

"Congratulations. I understand you got the old bag to come through with the eight hundred thousand. Don't forget your partner here. You owe me eighty thousand. Ten percent. And this time don't waste your money on the horses."

"That's nice," Whitney remarked sarcastically. "I wish I had a tape of that to take to the police. You're despicable." Then she walked out.

Eddie never showed up for the class again. That was three years ago. Then the dot-com he'd been asked to raise money for paid off handsomely for Lucretia. She moved to California, and he followed her.

He needed Lucretia. He needed her millions. He hadn't taken his buddy's advice, and once again he'd lost all his money at the track.

His apartment in Venice Beach was shoddy, at best. Unlivable, at worst. I hate this place, he thought, stepping into the shower and trying not to notice the mold and mildew. But I have to put up with this for only a couple more days if everything goes as planned. He lathered himself up and gave his hair a good shampoo. He couldn't stand all the gel he had to put in to give it the nerdy look. Once he and Lucretia were married, he'd slowly let her see his real appearance—the handsome one.

He laughed and thought again about how one presented oneself to the world made such a difference, about how appearances matter. Clothing, hairstyle, demeanor, attitude. If Lucretia ever saw "the real Eddie" wearing his psychedelic T-shirt and threadbare denim shorts, his hair wild and curly, dancing at the bar at the beach, she'd probably have a heart attack. He couldn't let her see that side of him. But then again, it bugged him that she thought he was a nerd. What had she said about not being interested in his type when he was younger? Huh! It just shows that she had no clue.

He wrapped a towel around his waist and went into the bedroom, which held his meager collection of earthly belongings. A lumpy mattress was graced by a scruffy quilt. He'd rented the apartment furnished. It had obviously been occupied by a number of tenants who didn't treat the place as lovingly as they would have if it were really their own.

In the closet hung his few good suits. The suits and his car were the most important tools of his trade. Show up in a nice car, especially in Los Angeles, look respectable, and you've won half the battle.

Within fifteen minutes Eddie was ready to leave the apartment, appearing for all the world like Lucretia Standish's respectable fiancé. But he wasn't heading straight to Beverly Hills. He had to go to the airport first.

He pulled up outside the baggage claim area at Terminal A at LAX. Eddie's friend had just called to say his plane had landed. And there he was, his partner in crime, Rex. Mr. Ten Percent.

After throwing his bag in the trunk, Rex opened the passenger door and started laughing. "You're a beaut," he said. "Nice hair. When's the bachelor party?"

Eddie put the pedal to the metal and pulled out abruptly.

"Hey, man, you didn't let me get my seat belt on," Rex protested. He was a big beefy guy in his mid-thirties, attractive in a thuggish kind of way. He had dirty blond hair, green eyes, and rugged features. His square jaw and broad nose could seem scary or cute, depending on his mood. When he wanted to, he could turn on the charm. When he didn't feel charming, his temper was bad.

They pulled out into the lane of cars exiting the airport.

"I'm telling you, Rex. I've finally hit the jackpot."

"And I get ten percent—which is what? I'd say about five million dollars. As of Sunday you'll be worth at least fifty million."

"Only if you find Freshness and keep her away until after the wedding."

"I'll do my best," Rex said, his voice suddenly deadly serious, which caused Eddie to glance over at him.

"I can't believe I took that stupid acting class in New York. Of all the luck. I'd be home free otherwise," Eddie moaned.

"Maybe, maybe not. You crossed a lot of people. Who's to say one of the other old ladies you 'advised' won't turn up somewhere along the way?"

Eddie waved his hand dismissively.

Rex shrugged. "So where's my new girlfriend's picture?"

Eddie reached down to his left and handed an envelope to Rex. It contained the picture he had taken from Lucretia's album.

"Not bad. She has that all-American girl-next-door look. Blond hair, freckles. Maybe I'll have to marry her."

"Not until next week," Eddie snapped.

"Take it easy. I know you're under pressure, but, please, I want your wedding day to be just perfect. Like you always dreamed of."

Eddie grunted and laughed slightly. "Sorry, Rex." He made a left turn off the main road leading from the airport and headed for the car rental area. "Now you're going to get yourself into one of those vehicles and drive up to the movie set near Santa Barbara. That's where she should be."

"Should be?"

"Where else would she be? Her mother told Lucretia she had a part in a film and was scheduled to be on location there for several weeks."

"That's all you know?"

"For now. Except the name of the movie. It's called *Jinxed*."

"Sounds like a winner."

Eddie pulled the car up to the rental office and stopped. "You've got her picture. You've got the address of the production office. I'm sure you can find our little Freshness."

"The thought of five million dollars does inspire the mind," Rex said nonchalantly as he opened the door. "Ta-ta. I'll be in touch." He got out, but then turned around and leaned back in. "It wouldn't hurt to see what else you can find out, partner."

"I'll be all ears," Eddie promised. "Do call and let me know you arrived safely."

Rex playfully hit the side of the car as Eddie drove off to Lucretia's, stopping only to pick up a dozen red roses.

5

———◆———

Regan drove up to her apartment in the Hollywood Hills above Sunset Boulevard. The small complex was quiet and peaceful. Birds were chirping, and the sun was rising in the clear blue sky.

In her comfortable two-bedroom apartment, Regan's suitcase was still on the floor, still unpacked. She threw a few clothes in a smaller bag and gathered her toiletries. The clock in her bedroom read 9:02.

She picked up the phone and dialed the number of the Four Seasons Hotel. A moment later her mother answered the phone in her room.

"Oh, hi, Regan. How's Jack?"

"About the same as last night, I suppose, Mom," Regan joked. "I dropped him off at the airport early this morning."

"I like him," Nora said solemnly.

"I know you do, Mom."

"It's a shame he had to get back early."

"Well, they needed him in New York. And now I have a new case."

"You do?"

"I'm heading up to the Santa Barbara area right now."

"Again?"

"I got a call this morning, and I'm off to find a girl who's working on a movie up there."

"You got a call already?"

"Yes. I've been to the office, and now I'm home getting ready to leave. I just wanted to let you know I won't be able to join you for dinner tonight."

"That's a shame. Wally and Bev were looking forward to seeing you."

Wally was a producer who had done a couple of Nora's television movies; Bev was his silent, long-suffering wife. Wally snapped his fingers a lot, usually to indicate lots of action happening on his movies, and further busied himself by chewing on a toothpick.

"I'm sorry to miss it," Regan said politely. "Something tells me I won't be back before dinner." She quickly explained the circumstances involving the missing girl.

"Two million each?" Nora gasped. "For going to the wedding?"

"Yes. How come there were no aunts like that in our family?" Regan teased.

"Good question. But don't forget Aunt Aggie left you that lovely hutch when she died. And those china dishes you can't get anywhere today."

"I'd rather have two million," Regan said matter-of-factly.

"I suppose," Nora agreed. "She was a silent film star, huh? Well, Regan, be careful. Here's Dad. He wants to say hello."

"Hi, Regan," Luke said heartily.

"Hi, Dad." Regan could just picture her parents in the suite at the Four Seasons having a room service breakfast. Six-foot-five Luke with his distinguished silver hair and his Jimmy Stewart good looks, and petite Nora with her blond hair and patrician face, probably wearing a silk robe. They were such a pair. The funeral director and the suspense writer who had spent more than thirty-five years together.

"How's Jack?" Luke asked.

Regan smiled. And after thirty-five years they thought alike. "Fine, Dad. I hope to see you sometime this weekend. But I have to head out of town on a case."

"I gather. Be careful, now."

"I will. I'll call you."

When Regan hung up the phone, she smiled again. She was lucky to have the parents she had.

In her car Regan straightened the rearview mirror, put on her sunglasses, and turned on the engine.

"Off in search of Freshness," she said aloud as she backed out of her parking space.

6

———◆———

Regan took 101, the inland route, to Unxta, the town near Santa Barbara where the movie was being filmed. Route 101 occasionally bordered the Pacific Ocean, and Regan couldn't believe that it was just yesterday she was experiencing these same sights with Jack as they drove along the Pacific Coast Highway.

When she saw the sign for Unxta, Regan pulled off the highway. She had called for directions and was told that the production office was located in the hotel where the cast and crew were staying. As Regan drove up the hilly road, past adobe houses with red-tiled roofs, she thought of how much she loved this area. Santa Barbara County was truly beautiful and diverse. Wineries, palm trees, great shopping, a temperate climate, and proximity to both the ocean and the mountains made for an attractive vacation spot or place to reside.

A little after eleven Regan pulled up to the hotel. It did not have a red tile roof or a charming exterior. What it did have was a neon sign that boasted cheap rooms with cable. But it looked respectable enough, and inside it was neat and clean. The desk clerk didn't seem to be in a hurry about anything, but he did eventually direct Regan around the corner and down the hall to where she would find the office for *Jinxed*.

At the door to the office, Regan knocked.

"Come in," someone shouted.

All right, already, Regan thought as she obeyed the command. Inside were four desks, all within inches of each other. Bulletin boards overflowed with lists, and a loud, impatient woman was on the phone. She hung up and turned to Regan.

"Hon, can I help you?" She seemed to be in her forties, with curly, brassy blond hair, a baseball cap, a pencil clinging to her ear, and a very determined manner.

"I hope so. I'm looking for Whitney Weldon."

"Whitney?" She picked up a clipboard on her desk and ran her finger down the page. "Like I thought, she's not working again until Monday." The clipboard dropped back down on the desk.

"Do you have any idea where she might be?" Regan inquired.

The woman looked at Regan incredulously. "Do you know how many actors I have to deal with? They get a few days off, they usually hit the road. This whole area is gorgeous. Some of them go to wineries, others to the beach; some spend the whole time in their room in misery. Don't ask me." The woman went back to her work.

"This is a family matter," Regan confided. "Whitney's mother needs to reach her, and she asked me to help find her." Regan tried to make it sound more meaningful than the fact that several million bucks was at stake. That might sound a little greedy. Then again, it might make this broad pay attention.

The woman sighed. She looked up at Regan. "You know what it's like to make a movie with temperamental actors? And this is low budget! The agents want this, the agents want that. I can't take it. One actor didn't like the car we picked him up in at the airport. Can you imagine? He's getting paid scale. He's no star!"

Regan clucked sympathetically. "A lot of tension, huh?"

"Tension, shmension. It's ri-dic-u-lous," she said, pronouncing each syllable with great deliberation. "Yesterday craft services put out chicken salad sandwiches that must have had lousy mayo because people are getting sick today. You can't leave food baking on the table on the set for hours. Let's see. What else can go wrong?" She shrugged and took a sip of her coffee. "By the way, what do you do? Are you a friend of Whitney's family?"

"I'm actually a private investigator."

The woman looked at Regan as though she were seeing her for the first time. "Oh, so you're like really serious. Would you like a cup of coffee?"

"I'd love one," Regan said, noticing the pot in the corner. "I'll get it." She walked over, picked up the pot, and poured what looked like day-old joe into an *Imus in the Morning* coffee mug. Regan smiled. Nora had appeared on Imus's radio show many times.

"Milk's in the fridge," the woman offered.

"Thanks." Regan leaned down and opened the tiny door. She pulled out a nearly empty carton of skim milk and drained it into her cup. She chucked the carton in a handy garbage and turned back around, getting a better view of a bulletin board with actors' pictures on it. Immediately she noticed Whitney. Whitney's mother had e-mailed a snapshot of her this morning. The photo on the board was a professional eight-by-ten, and Whitney looked beautiful.

The woman's eyes followed Regan's gaze. "There she is. You want a copy of it? I'll xerox it if you want."

"Thanks," Regan said as the woman got up and pulled out the thumbtack that was holding Whitney in place.

"Be right back." She walked into the adjoining room.

As Regan took a seat, she could hear the whir of the copying machine. I'm glad she wants to be helpful all of a sudden, Regan thought. It makes things easier.

A moment later Regan had in her hand a perfectly reproduced picture of Whitney Weldon, looking dramatic. The snapshot Regan had was of her smiling. Two different looks. Whitney probably had a few other headshots of herself, offering different moods in each one—serious, comic, perky, sexy. It depended on what role you were auditioning for.

"My name is Joanne," the woman said as she sat back down at her desk.

"And mine is Regan Reilly."

"Did you say Regan Reilly?"

"Yes, I did."

"Nora Regan Reilly's your mother?"

"Yes."

"I don't believe it. I worked on her last movie. She mentioned she had a daughter who was a private investigator."

"Oh, really," Regan said, smiling.

"Yeah. We filmed that one up around here, too."

"I remember. I never made it up to the set."

"It turned out pretty suspenseful."

"It did," Regan agreed.

"Tell your mother that Joanne says hi. She probably won't remember me."

"Oh, I bet she will," Regan assured her.

"We had a few laughs when she was here. It helps." She looked down at her desk. "Look at this mess."

"I know you're busy," Regan said quickly.

"It never stops when you work on these movies. Then when it's all over, you go home and crash."

"I can imagine. I'll just ask you a few questions."

"Sure. But don't worry. Relax. Drink your coffee."

"It's delicious," Regan lied.

"I'll help you out as much as I can, Regan. If I have to answer the phone or someone comes running in here hysterical about something or other, then I gotta stop. Ya know?"

"Absolutely. So what can you tell me about Whitney?"

"Nice kid. Mid-twenties. She's been in the business for a good five years. Funny actress. This is the biggest part she's ever had, and I think she's a little nervous about it."

"Really?"

"Well, I think so. I just sense it. She wants to do a good job. Yesterday her scenes didn't go very smoothly. It seemed like there was a bad vibe on the set. The assistant director kept howling for people to be quiet. It wasn't a great day."

"So she might have needed to escape from here," Regan suggested.

"I would if I had a few days off, believe me."

It's a big countryside out there, Regan thought. And Whitney isn't expected at her mother's until Sunday evening, more than forty-eight hours from now. She could be anywhere. "Are there any particular places where people hang out around here? Or where you think she might have gone?"

"She said she grew up not too far from here, so who knows? This area is so wonderful. There are so many things to do. It just depends on how much money you want to spend." Joanne paused, frowning. "I must admit to more than a passing curiosity as to why you need to find Whitney. Is anything wrong?"

Regan shook her head. "There's a family wedding this Sunday. Her mother really wants her to be there. It's important."

"Didn't she know about it before now?"

"No. It's an elderly aunt who just got engaged and doesn't want to wait to get married, so she's throwing it together for this weekend."

Joanne smiled. "Something tells me she must have a few bucks."

"I don't know about that," Regan said evasively.

Joanne waved her hand at Regan. "I had an aunt who everyone kissed up to for years. She left all her money to an animal shelter. We couldn't believe it. I mean we've got nothing against cats and dogs, but it was ri-dic-u-lous! Not a single cent to any of us who didn't bark or walk on four legs."

Regan laughed.

"It's true. I wouldn't break my neck to get to anybody's wedding these days. Big waste of time. If they want to leave you the money, they will. But the ones with the dough can usually spot phony baloney a mile away. By the way, who is she marrying?"

"I don't know him," Regan said honestly. "I've never met the bride or the groom. My job is to find Whitney."

Joanne tapped her fingers on the desk and readjusted her baseball cap. "Why don't you come to lunch with us? You can talk to people from the set. Maybe somebody can give you an idea of where she might have gone. I'm so busy in here, I don't spend much of what you'd call quality time with the actors."

"That'd be great," Regan said. "I really appreciate it. If any of them hear from her, they can ask Whitney to get in touch with me or her mother."

Joanne checked the massive watch on her tanned arm. "They'll be breaking in an hour. They're setting up lunch in a little park up the block from here. Why don't you meet me there?"

In other words, Regan thought, get out, I've got work to do. "Terrific," she said, then leaned forward and whispered conspiratorily. "I know that Whitney has a room at the hotel here. Her mother's been calling her all morning, but there's no answer. Do you think I could have a look in her room?"

Joanne gave her the hairy eyeball look. "Regan, I don't know."

In a hushed tone Regan explained, "I just want to see if there's anything in there that might indicate where she could have gone. You know, a brochure, a note, something. If you

34

want, I'll dial her mother's number right now so you can talk to her . . ."

Joanne put up her hand. "Don't bother. I'll give you a key. We keep spare keys to all the rooms in case the actor is on the set and forgot something." She crossed her eyes. "Like his script! Anyway, I'm sure it'll be all right for you to have a look around." She opened her drawer, consulted a list, and pulled out the key to room 178. "This must be some wedding," she mumbled as she handed it to Regan.

———◆———

7

When Edward arrived at the house, he was surprised to find that no one was home. Lucretia had given him a set of keys, and he let himself in. The rooms were cool and soothing. The house was decorated in a style that would not have been Edward's choice. Silently, he prayed that it wouldn't be too long before Lucretia went to her heavenly reward, and then he could go out and buy some masculine leather couches.

In the spotless kitchen overlooking the backyard, he found a crystal vase for the roses. On the counter he found a note in Lucretia's scrawly handwriting:

My darling Edward,

Phyllis and I have gone into town to do some shopping. I need a new dress for our big day! We'll be back for lunch. I miss you already.

Love,
Lucretia

"I can't wait," he said aloud as he filled the vase with water.

The phone on the wall rang. Eddie reached over and picked it up.

"Hello," he said quickly.

"Is Lucretia there?" a woman asked.

"No, she's not."

"This is Lilac Weldon, her niece. Who's this?"

Eddie swallowed hard. "This is Edward. How nice to talk to you."

"Oh, you, too. We're all looking forward to meeting you on Sunday."

"And I can't wait to meet Lucretia's family."

"Thank you. You know, I really don't need to speak to Lucretia," Lilac said. "You can help me. I'm buying a special wedding present, and I don't have your full name."

Oh, God, he thought. It's a good thing I changed my name. "Edward Fields."

"Any middle name?" Lilac asked.

"No. My parents weren't very imaginative."

"My daughter wishes I was less imaginative. Her name is Freshness, but in the outside world she goes by Whitney."

"Oh, that's funny," he said lightly as he grabbed hold of the countertop. "I hear she's an actress."

"Yes. And she's doing a movie now that could really be big for her. But she has taken off for the weekend. She likes to have days when she's out of touch. But I know she'd love to come to the wedding, so I've hired someone to track her down."

"You hired someone?"

"Yes. A private investigator named Regan Reilly. She's looking for her right now. I figured it's high time our family all got together, and this is the perfect occasion. I think Lucretia will be pleased if we all make it to the wedding."

"I know she will," Eddie said in a barely audible voice. "I'm sure she'll be overwhelmed that you went to the trouble of hiring a private detective."

"Please don't tell her. I want it to be a surprise. Regan's looking for Freshness at this very minute. And you know something? She's going to find her."

"Let's hope so."

"Edward, will your family be at the wedding?"

"No. I don't have a family."

"Awww," Lilac said tenderly. "I'm sure you'll have friends at the wedding. I'm looking forward to meeting them."

"Most of my friends are in New York," Edward practically stammered. "Everything's happening so fast that I don't think any of them will be able to make it. But Lucretia and I plan to visit there this summer."

"Where in New York?"

"The City," he said quickly. "Oh, there's another call coming in. We'll see you Sunday."

"Righto," Lilac replied.

Edward hung up the phone and closed his eyes to steady himself. He pulled out his cell phone and quickly dialed Rex.

"There are now two people you have to take care of," Edward informed Rex when he answered the phone. "The other one's name is Regan Reilly."

8

Phyllis and Lucretia drove into Beverly Hills with Phyllis at the wheel of Lucretia's Rolls-Royce. Phyllis used to drive the Rolls for her old employer as well. It was another one of the purchases Lucretia had made from the estate.

"Do you enjoy your work?" Lucretia asked Phyllis.

"Let me put it to you this way: If I won a lot of money on a game show, I'd quit!"

Lucretia laughed. "I'd miss you."

Phyllis glanced sideways at her employer. "You would?" She felt a pang of guilt about her call to Lilac. Not a big one, but a pang nonetheless.

"Yes. Absolutely. It's important to have people in your life whom you care about. And when you get to be my age, a lot of your friends are dead and gone."

"That's why it's good you invited your family to the wedding. Blood is thicker than water."

"They're not really my blood. They're Haskell's blood."

"Whatever," Phyllis mumbled as she turned down Rodeo Drive. "By the way, where's Edward's family?"

"He has none," Lucretia answered sadly.

"None? Everybody has a cousin hidden somewhere."

"I think it's too painful for him to talk about," Lucretia said simply as they passed one designer store after another.

Oh, brother, Phyllis thought as she checked her watch. She was missing her favorite show.

In Saks, Lucretia found a beaded pink dress with matching shoes.

"You look lovely," the salesgirls all told her.

"It's as good as it gets," Lucretia stated, smiling at her reflection. "Now, let's find something for Phyllis."

"I don't need anything," Phyllis protested.

"Yes, you do."

Fifteen minutes later, when Phyllis disappeared into the dressing room with a handful of dresses, the reverential saleswoman stared chatting with Lucretia. "I haven't seen you before. Have you lived here long?"

"Years ago, I lived here," Lucretia began. "I was a silent film star. It was such a wonderful life . . ."

By the time Phyllis had tried everything on and finally picked a handsome silk suit for the big day, Lucretia was wrapping up her life story. "I made millions on a dot-com, and now I'm getting married again."

"Husband number six. What a wonderful story. And to think you were a silent screen star. You're an inspiration to us all."

Lucretia smiled. "We're going down to pick up our marriage license this afternoon. And on Sunday I'll wear my beautiful dress from Saks."

As soon as Lucretia and Phyllis left the store with their purchases, the saleswoman picked up the phone. "I have a great piece of PR for us," she began.

9

Regan let herself into room 178, a plain, inexpensive hotel room with a double bed, small desk, ample-sized armoire with a television and several drawers, and two nightstands. Regan often felt deflated when she checked into one of these sterile hotel rooms. The sight of the brownish gray spread and curtains could make anyone's serotonin levels drop. Perhaps to counter that feeling Whitney had made this place her own. A couple of needle-point pillows were on the bed, framed pictures were on the desk, a colorful hat was perched on top of the armoire, and candles similar to the ones Regan had seen at Altered States abounded.

It wouldn't take long to look around.

A sliding glass door opened out over the hills toward the Pacific. The room might not be the most luxurious, but the view was great.

Regan sat at the desk and picked up one of the pictures. It was Whitney and Lilac. They looked so much alike. Another photo showed Whitney standing between two men who looked as if they were related. Lilac had mentioned that Whitney was close to her two uncles, explaining that Whitney's father was a flake who had taken off when she was a baby. No one had heard from him in years.

Regan pulled open the desk drawer. There was a copy of the script *Jinxed*. On the front page the name "Judy" was written in red. Regan flipped through the script and noted that all of the character Judy's lines were highlighted. If she went away for a few days, I'm surprised that she didn't bring the script with her, Regan thought.

Regan pulled the drawer open a bit more and discovered an address book and a day planner. She opened the planner to today's date, and of course it was blank. On Sunday was Mother's Day. A brief survey of the other pages didn't provide any other information, but a piece of paper in the back of the book fell out. Regan read, "Things to do."

1. Get Mom a good present for Mother's Day. Pottery?
2. Skin cream
3. Vitamins
4. GET CALM

Wow, Regan thought. When did she write this list? A quick look through the remaining drawers revealed nothing unusual. Regan found a big empty suitcase in the closet. Toiletries were in the bathroom, but there was no sign of a toothbrush or toothpaste.

On her way out Regan spotted a magazine that had fallen between the bed and the nightstand: *Destinations and Diversions*. Inside were a lot of notations next to ads for restaurants, hotels, and spas in central California. "I'm sure you don't mind if I borrow this, Whitney," Regan said aloud. "I just hope it helps me find you."

The clock radio on the table read 12:15.

Time for lunch, Regan thought as she exited the room.

10

⸺◆⸺

Whitney Weldon had had a rough week. She'd gotten involved with the director, Frank Kipsman, and they had to keep it secret until the movie was finished. She was so worried about doing a good job, and Frank was worried because they were running out of money. And her agent had phoned her to say she'd just lost out on another part to an actress who, it seemed, would always be getting in her way.

Last night she'd driven out to the beach, headed north, and checked into a little motel right on the water. This morning she'd slept late and then walked the beach restlessly. She needed to get centered. Her thoughts kept returning to the career seminar that Ricky, one of the production assistants, had mentioned. He said there was a great program at a retreat in the hills on Saturday. It was something along the lines of EST and only for actors. There were only a few spaces left, so he told her not to tell anybody else. At first she balked, but her mind kept coming back to the seminar.

Maybe I should go, she thought. Maybe it will help me. I have nothing else to do, and Frank is heading down to Los Angeles to try to raise money for the film. Whitney dug in her purse for the number Ricky had given her. She stared at the little piece of paper for several moments. Did she want to be that vulnerable? Whitney imagined that she'd be better known than any of the other actors there.

But she'd just missed out on a big part.

Grabbing the cell phone from the bottom of her purse, she turned it on. She dialed the number of the seminar and actually talked to the guy who was running it. He was a director and screenwriter, and sounded so pleased that she'd be joining them. The seminar would cost $500 and end Sunday morning. That would be perfect. She shut off her phone, not bothering to check the messages.

"Good," she said aloud. "I've taken a positive step." She had half a mind to go back to the hotel in Unxta and spend the night. It was closer to the retreat, and she could pick up some comfortable clothing. Many of these kinds of seminars had you sitting on the floor all day.

Nah, I want to stay away from that vibe. I'll stay right here, she decided, as she stared out at the churning waters of the Pacific.

11

A full luncheon buffet was ready in the park for the cast and crew of *Jinxed*. The table was filled with everything from salad to macaroni to sandwich makings. Hot dogs and hamburgers were on the grill. Fruit, cookies, and candy were on display. Five minutes after the last scene of the morning was finished, a long line had formed at the buffet table.

Regan walked up the block to the park and spotted Joanne.

"Over here, Regan," she waved.

Regan made her way to Joanne's table in the shade, amazed as always at how many people work on a movie set. It was a beautiful day, and everyone seemed glad to be outside. The tables were filling up, and the barbecue was smoking. Regan wondered how many vegetarians were in the bunch and if they were offended by the smell of the grilled meat.

"Regan, would you like some lunch?" Joanne asked.

"Thanks. I'll wait till the line gets shorter."

A sixtyish woman with striking red hair, wearing black stretch pants, a white overblouse, and sneakers, came barreling over to the table. Big earrings and an oversized pair of glasses completed the look. Regan could tell immediately that she wasn't a shrinking violet.

"I'm Molly. I do makeup."

"Hi, Molly."

"Joanne told me you're looking for Whitney. Is everything all right?"

"Yes, I think so," Regan answered honestly. "A family wedding came up, and they'd like her to be there on Sunday, so I'm trying to find her."

Molly pushed the glasses back on her nose. "I know yesterday she wasn't very happy." She sat down on the bench next to Regan. "When you do people's makeup, you get close. You talk. She mentioned something about really wanting to work on her acting, that she really wanted to learn how to 'let go.' Not that she's not good now. I really think she's going to be a star."

"Do you know if she takes any acting classes?" Regan asked.

"Yes. She said she studies with a guy named Clay Ruleman in Beverly Hills. A lot of the actors I've worked with swear by him."

"I bet she wouldn't have gone down there for the weekend," Regan mused.

"She might have. He has a Saturday class."

"It's worth checking out," Regan said.

"Whitney also likes to hike. She finds it very relaxing."

Oh, great, Regan thought. Finding a hiker in California is like finding a needle in a haystack.

Over a hot dog and a Coke, the only other thing Regan learned was that the hotel bar was where the movie people would congregate for a drink. Whitney had stopped by a couple of times for a glass of wine, but she always went to bed early. It was obvious that Whitney was nervous about doing a good job on the film—it was her first lead role—and she'd gone away for the weekend to relax.

Regan handed out numerous cards with her cell phone number on it and asked, "If anyone sees or hears from Whitney, please have her call me."

Back in her car, Regan picked up her cell phone and asked information for Clay Ruleman's studio. A minute later she learned there was no Saturday class this week. Clay was out of town.

Regan started the car. She drove past the house where the filming was taking place. Inside, Frank Kipsman was eating his lunch alone. He had no idea she was looking for Whitney.

12

Rex had rented the most nondescript SUV with the darkest tinted windows allowable by law. He would have preferred a convertible so he could soak up a few rays, but he knew that on this job he'd have to keep as low a profile as possible. As he headed up the highway toward Unxta, Rex started to get a little anxious. Five million dollars. That's how much he'd get if he kept Whitney Weldon away until after the wedding on Sunday.

Rex laughed nervously. Boy, did Eddie luck out. This was the biggest deal ever. And it was a fluke that old Lucretia had made so much money off that dot-com. If she hadn't pulled out, she would have lost her whole investment like so many others who had put their money into the company. Rex couldn't believe that all Eddie had been hired to do was find investors—one of his only honest jobs. Who would have guessed that he'd reap such benefits while the whiz kids who hired him were now wiped out? Wait until they found out that Eddie was about to get a permanent seat on the gravy train, all thanks to their business that was now kaput.

Running his hand through his hair, Rex sighed. How many years would Eddie have to put in before Lucretia kicked the bucket? Hell, for another five million he'd take care of things.

It took less than two hours to reach the town of Unxta. Rex headed straight for the hotel that housed the *Jinxed* production office. I'll have a little lunch at the hotel and see what I can find out, he thought. But when he was about to turn into the hotel parking lot, Rex noticed a caravan of movie trucks parked up the street.

He steered the SUV up the block. "Someone's having a picnic," he muttered as he took in the setup in the park. Rex grabbed the nearest parking space, rolled down the window, and turned off the motor. He was just in time to hear a woman with a baseball cap tell another woman that a Regan Reilly would be here for lunch and she was looking for Whitney Weldon. He couldn't believe his luck. Regan Reilly was the private investigator.

I'll wait until she gets here, he thought. Then I'll tail her and see what she's doing to find Whitney. And if she does find her, then I'll nab both of them. Whitney Weldon and Regan Reilly would have to disappear together. Rex laughed. Old Eddie would really be getting two for the price of one.

A few minutes later a young, dark-haired woman who turned out to be Regan Reilly appeared. Rex got out and sat on a bench near the sidewalk, as close as possible to where Reilly was having her lunch. When she left the park, he got in his car and followed her. He didn't intend to let her out of his sight.

13

————◆————

Regan sat in her car and thumbed through the copy of *Destinations and Diversions* she had taken from Whitney's room. It was a local travel magazine hyping hotels, restaurants, recreational activities, and beaches. Santa Barbara County had one hundred miles of outstanding California coastline. Whitney had circled the section on beaches and had exclamation points next to every beach mentioned. That really narrows it down, Regan thought as she grimaced. Frustrated, she put the magazine down on the seat.

In the hotel parking lot, everything was quiet. It was midafternoon, the time of day when it was hot and energy levels dropped. Regan remembered that in the summertime when she was a kid, she'd splash around in the local pool all afternoon, never getting tired. As an adult you have to forge through the heat of the day. It would be nice to sit in the shade with a nice glass of lemonade, Regan thought.

She got out her legal pad and started to make notes. Whitney was worried about her performance. She wanted to work on her acting. Her mother said she liked to go on these weekends by herself. Go with the flow. Regan had tried that a couple of times but always ended up going home to her apartment and calling a friend to get together for dinner. She'd spent enough time alone working on her cases. And after growing up as an only child, Regan preferred to be alone in her apartment rather than on the road where everyone else seemed to be with a group.

But if someone wanted to be alone, where would they go?

She had a hunch that Whitney would have headed to the beach.

Regan turned on the engine, proceeded out of the parking lot, and headed back to the highway. Whitney would go north, Regan thought. That's where she had to end up on Sunday. She probably wouldn't have headed back in the direction of Los Angeles.

Regan took Route 1 and stopped at a dozen hotels and motels along the way. None of the guests anywhere was registered as Whitney Weldon. Regan started compiling a list. She called Lilac and told her that she wanted to come up and get some help from her and her brothers in calling all the hotels and motels listed in the travel magazine.

At 5:00 Regan once again found herself traveling down the bumpy road to the winery. All was quiet when she arrived. Inside the lodge Lilac was behind the reception desk. She got up to greet Regan and once again looked like Mother Earth with her peasant blouse, long flowing skirt, and clodhopper sandals.

"Wow. I'm so glad you're here, Regan. Earl and Leon are dying to meet you. Let me get them."

Lilac ran off, and Regan got a chance to look around more thoroughly than she had the day before. The main lodge was certainly handsome. It had a rustic feeling. Large windows overlooked the vineyards and softly rolling hills. Glass doors opened onto a large deck. The bedrooms were located at one end of the reception hall, and the dining room at the other.

Ten minutes later, Regan, Lilac, Leon, and Earl were seated on the back deck, with lemonade glasses in their hands.

"Are you sure you don't want some of our wine?" Leon asked. "We have a stunning pinot noir and a wonderful, buttery chardonnay."

"Later," Regan promised.

The two brothers appeared to be completely opposite types. Leon was in tight jeans and a T-shirt, and had a macho appearance. His skin was deeply tanned, his hair was dark, and he sported a rather bushy mustache. His body was muscular and compact, and looked as if he spent a lot of time doing physical labor. Earl, on the other hand, was tall, thin, and angular. His head was shaved, and he was wearing what could have passed as gauzy cotton pajamas and a pair of flip-flops.

It's amazing, Regan thought, the different types who come from the same parents. She wondered what a brother or sister of hers would have been like.

And there was no mistaking that Lilac had been a hippie in her day. She had long straight blond hair flecked with gray, wore no makeup, and looked like an ad for granola. Her attractiveness was otherworldly. Regan could imagine her twenty-five years ago naming her newborn child Freshness. All three siblings were baby boomers now in their fifties.

"It's pretty amazing," Regan said. "The three of you living and working all together."

"It's always been my dream to have a winery," Leon told Regan. "I like to work with dirt."

"Uh-huh." Regan nodded her head.

"Our grandfather over in Italy made wine in the bathtub. From what I understand, it didn't win any medals for taste, but he loved it. When my mother moved to this country with my father, whom she met during World War II, she was always sending pictures of the California vineyards to my grandfather in Italy. Grandpa came to visit a couple of times before he died. I can still hear him saying, 'Leon, the best thing you can do is work the land. Feel the dirt in your fingers.' "

The grapes between your toes, Regan thought.

"Trouble is, I had a job as a tree trimmer and was making pretty good money. I was married at the time and had a wife to support. I didn't have enough to buy a decent vineyard. Then a few years ago I saw a notice that this place was going on the auction block. It's supposedly haunted. It's not very big, but it was cheap! I couldn't believe it. I couldn't swing it on my own, so I persuaded my brother and sister to invest in it with me. We inherited a little bit of money when our parents died."

Earl and Lilac smiled at their brother.

"Earl's got the meditation stuff going. Lilac runs the gift shop and the tastings and the bed-and-breakfast. We want this place to be a nice boutique winery that's a little different, a 'get-away-from-it-all kind of place,' you know?"

Regan nodded.

"But it costs a lot of money. We owe taxes. Equipment that was supposed to be good has broken down. Buying furniture is expensive. We want to remodel the barn at the edge of the property that has nothing but junk in it. And a winery down the block is upset this place is back in business."

"Really?" Regan asked with surprise.

"Yeah. Up in the Napa Valley there are tons of wineries, but they got tons of tourists. So it works out okay. But even they are having problems. Environmentalists don't want the vineyards cutting down any more trees. Some people think Napa is becoming too popular for its own good. The state of California is producing a glut of wine that is pushing down the prices."

"I didn't realize that," Regan said.

Leon gestured with his hands. "What are you gonna do? I'm still glad we bought this place. Down here the wine country is not as famous, and that's the way we like it. Altered States is perfect for us. We thought we'd eventually build little cottages for ourselves on the property. If one of us ever gets married, we'll have our privacy."

"That'll be the day," Earl chimed in. "The divorce rate in this family is way above the national average."

Regan chuckled. "Were there a lot of bidders at the auction?"

"No. That's what was surprising. I thought there would have been more."

"And now that you've gotten things going—" Regan stopped in midsentence as Earl stood up and bent over, touching his toes. The other two didn't even blink.

Earl straightened up and started stretching out his arms. "It has been said that wine promotes well-being, aids digestion, and calms the soul. So does meditation. That's why we offer both here."

"Sounds good," Regan said.

"My brother and I are very different," Earl continued as he rotated his head in half circles back and forth.

"Sit down, Earl," Leon snapped.

Earl sat on the floor and assumed the lotus position.

Leon glared at his brother. He looks as if he wants to kill him, Regan thought. They always say that it's not easy for families to be in business together.

"We're so happy here," Lilac said sweetly in an obvious attempt to smooth things over. "We're all different, but we thought it would be great to honor our grandfather and form a sort of commune. In Italy when Grandpa was growing up, families lived together in little villages. We don't have that here, so we thought we'd start one. Our guests and friends are the villagers."

No wonder Whitney took off for the weekend, Regan thought.

Earl's watch beeped. He unfolded his legs, stood up, and announced, "Time for a vitamin shake."

"Wait a minute," Leon insisted. "Let's finish this meeting. It's important for the future of this place that we find Whitney."

Earl nodded almost imperceptibly. Somehow Regan didn't think he was much help to Leon out in the vineyards. And somehow she couldn't imagine Leon in a meditation session. No, Leon was the physical, down-to-earth type, and Earl was the spiritual one with his head in the clouds. Lilac was a little of both.

"From what Lilac tells me, you stand to get a lot of money for showing up at Lucretia's wedding."

"It's absolutely unbelievable," Leon said strongly. "Why doesn't she just give us the money?"

"Leon," Lilac challenged. "Why should she? We've never bothered with her."

Leon turned to Earl. "I wish you had never encouraged Whitney's go-with-the-flow weekends. We should be able to reach her at all times."

"She needs space," Earl said simply.

"Okay," Regan interjected quickly. "I went to the movie set. I gather Whitney was a little worried about the work she's been doing this week."

"She's a very good actress," Lilac interrupted. "She's very funny."

"I gather," Regan said. "And this part could be a breakthrough for her. In any case, she's gone from the movie set for the weekend, and our goal is to get her to Lucretia's garden for the wedding on Sunday morning. What I'd like to do is have us start phoning hotels and motels in Santa Barbara County and see if she's registered."

Earl looked at his watch. "My no-talking hour is between six and seven P.M. daily."

"Then you can go through the yellow pages and guidebooks during that time and make a list of hotels for us to call."

"That I can do."

Alleluia, Regan thought. "Do you have any guests this weekend whom you'll have to attend to?" she asked the trio.

"No." Lilac said, smiling. "We had three couples coming from New York for a wedding, but the bride got cold feet and called it off. So they canceled. You and your friend Jack Reilly would have been here alone with us."

Boy, do I wish he was here, Regan thought. She couldn't wait to talk to him. He's the one who found the listing for Altered States in some obscure guidebook. "I have to go out to my car to get a few things," she said. She'd also place a quick call to Jack.

"Let's meet in the office in five minutes," Lilac suggested. "There are several phone lines in there."

"I'll be right back," Regan announced as she got up and stepped over Earl's now outstretched legs. This guy has the potential to be a real nudge, she thought. It's *because* of people like him that others need meditation.

"Excuse me," he said, pulling his legs in, nearly tripping Regan in the process.

"No problem," she answered, regaining her balance. She almost laughed. She was suddenly glad that at least he'd keep his mouth shut for the next hour. Too bad they couldn't tie him up as well.

If only Jack were here, he'd get such a kick out of this. She'd tell him it was all his fault for buying that guidebook. Quickening her pace, she hurried out to the car.

14

Lucretia came back to the house as giddy as a school-girl. "You can't see my dress," she cried to Edward. "It's a surprise."

"Whatever you wear, I know you will look beautiful," Edward assured her.

She had found him in the backyard, sunning himself by the pool. "I want to have a good tan," he explained, "so I will be your handsome groom."

"I know you'll do your best to look handsome on Sunday," Lucretia said gently. "And in my eyes you will."

Eddie felt slighted by the remark but cheered himself with the thought of more than $50 million.

Across the fence in the next yard, old-time movie star Charles Bennett was tending to his roses. He glanced over and saw Lucretia sitting there with Edward. Charles didn't like the looks of that young guy at all. He'd talked to Lucretia a couple of times over the fence, and she'd called to invite him to her wedding on Sunday.

The quick wedding seemed very suspicious. Lucretia was a lovely lady, a few years older than Charles, and she seemed to be captivated by this Svengali. It wasn't right, but it was none of his business. He went back to his roses.

"We have to go downtown and pick up our marriage license," Lucretia reminded Edward. "But first Phyllis will fix us a little lunch."

They ate at stools in the kitchen, Lucretia's tiny feet dangling in midair. Phyllis had reluctantly turned off the television when she served them their sandwiches.

"Don't you have *any* friends you want to invite to the wedding?" Lucretia asked Edward.

"I'm going to be so nervous," Edward told her. "I'd rather have a big party in a month or two, after we've settled in. We can show everyone how wonderful married life is."

Phyllis almost gagged as she poured iced tea into their glasses.

"I've always loved having big weddings," Lucretia said. "My first three were huge affairs with hundreds of people, although I must admit the last couple were quiet. I have to give the caterer a final count. I sent invitations to a few of the neighbors."

"You did?" Edward questioned, sounding alarmed.

"Yes, darling. Why not?"

"We don't know them."

"Well, now we will. They're our neighbors. I want to shout to the world that we're getting married and invite everyone to our party."

Edward felt the onslaught of the worst stomachache of his life.

"And I so hope the kids can make it."

"Something tells me they will," Phyllis stated matter-of-factly.

"You think so?" Lucretia said gaily.

"I'd be willing to bet on it."

Edward glared at her, then turned to Lucretia. "Whenever you're ready . . ."

Lucretia jumped off her chair. "Let's go."

There was a camera crew waiting at the town clerk's office in Beverly Hills.

"Lucretia Standish?" a female reporter asked.

"That's me!" Lucretia said, smiling, clearly enjoying the attention.

"I'm from GOS news. We're doing a story on special couples getting married in the month of May. We heard you were shopping for your wedding dress today at Saks. Congratulations!"

"Thank you." Lucretia beamed, posing for the camera.

"We also heard you made a fortune from an investment in a dot-com, so at this stage of your life you're not only in the money but you're in love."

"I am so in love! And this is my fiancé . . ." Lucretia turned to her right.

Edward was gone. He had disappeared down the hallway.

Lucretia turned back to the reporter. "He's so shy. It's his first wedding. My sixth, his first."

"What a great story."

"Wonderful!" Lucretia exulted. "When will it be on?"

"It will be on the evening news tonight, and we'll probably rerun the segment this weekend."

"Would you like to come to the wedding?" Lucretia asked. "It's this Sunday at noon in my garden. It's going to be lovely."

"I'll be there," the reporter assured her, writing down the address. "But now I'd like to ask you a few questions about how you knew to get out of the dot-com before it went bankrupt and how you knew you were in love."

"Well, you see," Lucretia began, patting her hair, "I knew I was always destined to make millions . . ."

15

The young production assistant felt as if he wanted to die. Food poisoning had robbed Ricky of what felt like all the fluids in his body. Retching and wretched, he clung to his bed in the hotel.

There were probably only two sandwiches that were bad. How did I manage to grab one of them? he wondered miserably. He reached over for the glass on his night table and slowly brought the now-warm ginger ale to his lips. Delicately, very delicately, he sipped. He knew his system couldn't take too much of a jolt. Even a sip of ginger ale could be dangerous.

The phone—that was now just inches from his head—rang. The loud piercing sound suddenly made his headache unbearable. As quickly as he could, he picked up the receiver.

"Hello."

"Ricky?"

"Yeah."

"Norman here. You sound terrible."

"I feel terrible. I ate something bad. I must have food poisoning."

"I hate that."

"Me, too." Ricky closed his eyes and held his hand to his forehead.

"Listen, I wanted to thank you. Whitney Weldon called. She's coming to the seminar tomorrow."

"Great. You owe me a hundred bucks. I'm not surprised she called you."

"Why?"

"A lot of reasons. She and the director, a guy named Frank Kipsman, have a thing going. She really wants to do a good job on his movie, and she wants to be confident. Plus I overheard them talking. They're running out of money, which is too bad. The truth is that this would be a good breakout film for both of them. Kipsman is really stressed-out."

"They're running out of money?"

"Yup. They had just enough to start filming, and some other money hasn't come through yet. They'll have to close up if they don't get more money soon. I think Kipsman is going down to L.A. to try to raise money this weekend. Nobody really knows that Whitney is involved with Kipsman, and nobody knows how bad the financial situation is."

"Except you."

"You know me—I always have my ear to the ground. I heard Kipsman tell Whitney to get away for the weekend. That's why I thought she'd be interested in the seminar."

On the other end of the phone, Norman sighed. "So she's involved with Kipsman, huh?"

"They've got that look. She told him she wished she had the money to give him to save the movie."

"How romantic."

"Yeah."

"All right. Go drink some ginger ale. If you find somebody else who wants to gain their confidence this weekend, send them right over."

"A hundred bucks apiece."

"The check's in the mail." Norman hung up.

Ricky rolled over and assumed the fetal position. Thank God it's Friday, he thought. I won't have to get out of this bed for three days.

16

Regan went out to her car, her office on wheels, and called Jack. He had just left the office.

"I miss you," he said, his voice full of affection. "Are you home?"

"No," Regan said, smiling.

"Are you in the car?"

"Well, yes. But it's not moving."

"Are you broken down? I'd love to help, but I'm three thousand miles away."

"I'm not broken down. And don't remind me that you're so far away."

Jack laughed. "Am I supposed to keep guessing your whereabouts? Is this the game of Twenty Questions?"

Regan chuckled. "I will keep you on the edge of your seat no longer." She cleared her throat and lowered her voice. "I'm sitting in the driveway of the winery we almost stayed at last night."

"Are you kidding me?" Jack said. "You miss me so much that you had to go back?"

"I had to go back and recapture our fleeting moments together."

"Are they charging for the accommodations after all? You decided to make use of them?"

"No! They're actually paying me to stay here."

"Do tell, my dear," Jack said as a broad grin spread across his face. When Regan was finished, he just shook his head and laughed. "I suppose it is my fault for finding Altered States in the guidebook. But you do surprise me. I'm sitting on an airplane all day thinking you're still taking it easy, and there you are back to work, back on the road."

"If we stayed here last night, we'd probably be working on this together."

"I must say it's an unusual case for either one of us to work on—to find someone so she can go to a wedding and collect two million dollars."

"I know it's not a matter of life or death," Regan said, "but to these people the money is very important."

A feeling of unease came over Jack. "I must say I don't like it when you say it's not a matter of life or death. That makes me think that somehow it'll turn out to be just that."

"I'll be fine," Regan assured him. "But do me a favor, if you don't mind. See if you can find out anything about Lucretia Standish. I just have a hunch it might be helpful."

"Will do," Jack said as another call beeped into his phone. "I'll talk to you later. Be careful."

Regan smiled. Jack was always worried about her. It felt good. "You provide the most excitement in my life," she told him.

"Let's keep it that way."

17

$\diamond$

Whitney felt a restlessness that wouldn't go away. After walking on the beach for hours, she went back to her room at the motel and started running the water for a bath. She poured in some special calming aromatherapy bath salts her mother had given her and then turned to look at herself in the mirror. I look tired, she thought. I'm too worried. I'm worried about my acting, about Frank, and about the movie being shut down.

Whitney wished she could have gone to Los Angeles with Frank, but it was too soon for them to be seen together. They had just hooked up when he cast her in the film. Frank didn't want them talking on the set, thinking he wasn't serious, thinking it was just a fling. He was already under a lot of pressure and didn't need any more.

It was basically your typical office romance that had to be kept quiet. Just the setting was different.

Heck, Whitney thought as she stepped into the steamy tub and felt herself beginning to relax. They say the best way to meet somebody is at work. It's getting to the safe place where you're really a couple that is the hard part. If you break up, it's sticky business, especially if you have to face that person every day.

The tub wasn't the biggest, but it held enough water to do the trick. She closed her eyes and started going over everything in her mind. *Jinxed.* Some title for a movie. She only hoped it didn't turn out to be prophetic. No, Frank would get the money to finish the film.

For fifteen minutes Whitney lolled in the hot, bubbly water. Here I am on another one of my "go-with-the-flow" weekends, she thought. But somehow it didn't feel right. She didn't want to be alone. She suddenly stood and reached for one of the thin white towels that felt as fluffy as flattened cardboard. Hurriedly, she dried herself off and got dressed in a pair of jeans and a cotton sweater. It was nearly seven o'clock, and she had made a decision.

I'll check out of this place and go home to the winery. I feel like being with my mother and whoever else is around. We'll have a glass of wine and talk, and I know I'll feel better. And tomorrow I'll get up early and leave for the seminar—it's not far from Altered States.

She threw her few things in a bag and looked around the room to make sure she hadn't forgotten anything.

At the checkout desk the clerk looked surprised. "I thought you were staying until tomorrow," he said, peering at her over his glasses.

"My plans have changed," she said simply.

"I still have to charge you for tonight. You stayed past noon today, and, you know, I could have given the room to somebody else."

"It's okay."

"Didn't I see you in some movie?" the clerk continued, frowning in concentration. "I think I did."

"I've done a few movies," Whitney replied, wishing he would just check her out quickly.

"I knew it! You played a funny part. . . . I'm trying to think of what the name of it was."

"I usually do comedy," Whitney said as politely as she could.

"Can I have your autograph?" he asked, handing her a piece of paper with the hotel's name on it.

"Sure. What's your name?"

"Herman."

Whitney scrawled "To Herman. Best wishes. Whitney Weldon" and handed it back to him.

He squinted at it. "Could you put today's date on it?"

"Sure."

As Whitney wrote the date, he took her credit card and printed out her bill. When she signed the receipt, he joked, "Now I have your autograph twice. But I think the credit card company wants this one more than I do." He started to laugh, a wheezing, snorting sound that initially grated on Whitney. As he continued, she started to laugh as well, which made him repeat the joke again.

"Yup, they want your autograph more than I do," he said for the third time.

He took forever to fold up her bill and stuff it in an envelope. "Do come back and join us again, Ms. Weldon. Pretty soon you'll be a big movie star, and I can say I knew you when."

By this time Whitney couldn't get out of there fast enough. "Thank you," she said as she picked up her bag and hightailed it out the door and into the parking lot.

The clerk smiled to himself, then suddenly realized he hadn't handed her back her credit card. He trudged as fast as he could, following her footsteps, but when he got out to the parking lot, it was too late. There was no sign of her. She was gone, headed one way or the other on the Pacific Coast Highway.

"Tsk, tsk, tsk," he said aloud. "Now that's a shame." Back

into the motel he went, finding the lobby just as empty as before. The ring of the telephone broke the silence. He hurried over to answer it.

"Pacific Waters Motel," he answered in an eager chirpy tone.

"Huh?" he said a moment later. "Well, you're not going to believe this. She checked out no more than two minutes ago.... No, she's gone. I tried to chase after her. She left her credit card here. Isn't that a shame? My fault, really. I didn't hand it back to her. If she comes back, I'll definitely have her call her mother. By the way, she's a lovely actress."

On the other end of the phone Regan conveyed the news to the group. Lilac and Leon groaned while Earl made a face. It wasn't seven o'clock yet, so no sounds were allowed.

"She just left!" Lilac cried. "I don't believe it!"

Leon pounded the table with his fist and then glared at Earl. Regan knew what he was thinking. If Earl had been helping with the phone calls this hour, they would have reached the motel before Whitney checked out.

"Now we don't know where she's going. She might even be heading for one of the places we already called!" Lilac cried in despair. "We'll have to start all over again!"

"We may as well stop calling for now," Regan said. "She's on the road, and I imagine she must be planning to drive at least a bit of a distance or she wouldn't have checked out."

"Who knows where she's going," Leon said with disgust.

Earl's watch beeped. "Seven o'clock," he proclaimed as he rejoined the speakers of the world. "I think we'll find her. The universe will send her to us."

"I'll phone the clerk again and ask him to make sure whoever is on duty this weekend knows it's vital that Whitney call home. Let's hope she contacts them about her credit card," Regan said, trying to be positive.

As Lilac nodded, she switched on the television in the office. The news was coming on, trumpeting the headlines of the day.

"And later," the anchor was saying, "we'll talk to you about May weddings. It's a big month for marriage, and we have a piece on a special May-to-December romance. Ladies, go for it! We'll introduce you to a woman who was a silent film star. Lucretia Standish is getting married for the sixth time, and her lucky husband is a much younger man."

"Oh my God!" Lilac cried. "There she is!"

A much younger man, Regan thought. How much younger?

"If she's marrying a younger guy," Leon noted astutely, "he'll take control of her money. We can kiss good-bye any chance of getting those millions if we don't all get to the wedding."

I'd say he's right about that, Regan thought.

Earl finally made himself useful. He exited, then came back carrying a bottle of pinot noir and a tray with four glasses. Regan was surprised at how deft he was as he uncorked the bottle and poured with finesse. She noticed that the label had the sketch of an old man standing in a pile of grapes in the bathtub. I guess that's Grandpa, she thought.

Leon's face remained impassive. He accepted his glass and took a big gulp.

What money will do to us, Regan thought. Gaining it, losing it, coming close to a bonanza. It makes everybody crazy.

"I can't believe that Whitney won't call that motel before Sunday," Regan found herself saying. "If she goes to another motel, she'll need her credit card."

"She has several credit cards," Lilac said flatly. "When things get really tight, she rotates them, borrowing cash from different ones. Her credit is good, but I know she won't use the same card two times in a row."

Oh, great, Regan thought as she sipped the "Grandpa" wine.

She didn't know why she was surprised, but it actually tasted good. She wished the segment on Lucretia would start quickly.

"So you never met Lucretia," she remarked to the unhappy threesome.

They all looked guilty.

"We were busy . . ." Lilac began just as the anchor's face once again filled the screen.

"Meet Lucretia Standish."

They watched as ninety-three-year-old Lucretia gaily told of her plans to marry on Sunday. "My husband-to-be is so shy," she said as a shot of Edward Fields, fleeing down the hallway outside of the civil offices in Beverly Hills, filled the screen.

"He moves fast," Regan noted.

"He certainly does," Leon agreed. "Something about it smells."

"And there's nothing we can do about it," Earl said. "If we knew Lucretia better, we might be able to, but not now."

Edward Fields, Regan thought. She'd ask Jack to check that name as well. If Regan's instincts were correct, Lucretia Standish would be in big trouble if she said "I do" to that bird.

As the foursome stared at the television, they had no idea that they were under surveillance by a big lurking guy named Rex, whose alias was Don Lesser.

18

Rex had followed Regan to the dirt road leading to the winery. A big sign said ALTERED STATES WINERY. Another sign said DEEP BREATHS MEDITATION CENTER. He hadn't dared follow any farther in his car. How could he possibly hide? But he knew that this was where Whitney Weldon's mother lived.

Rex had bought a dark wig, and he'd put in his colored contacts. He was still recognizable as a big fellow, but now his hair was black and his eyes were brown. Anything to look different.

He drove a short way down the road, then did a U-turn, pulled over, rolled down the windows, and turned off the car. The vineyards and rolling hills were beautiful. It was late afternoon, and the light was softening. He loved this time of day. It meant night was not far off. For Rex nighttime was when he felt most himself. If there was one thing Rex wasn't, it was a morning person.

He picked up his cell phone and called Eddie.

"I'm outside the winery."

"Just a minute."

Rex could tell that Eddie was turning away from the phone.

"Excuse me, Lucretia," he apologized. "This is about a surprise for you."

73

He's got that partially right, Rex thought.

"Okay," Eddie said finally. "I'm out of earshot."

"I followed Regan Reilly up here to the winery where Whitney's mother lives."

"How did you find her so fast?"

"She was at the movie set. Anyway, I'm going to see if they have a room for the night."

"Don't you think that's a little dangerous?"

"Yes, but at least I'll have my finger on the pulse of what they're doing to find Whitney. How are things with you?"

"Lucretia wants to tell the world about this wedding. I'd love to give her a couple of sleeping pills so she doesn't wake up until Sunday."

"Not a bad idea."

"The maid's always around. She'd know something was up."

"I guess." Rex tapped his fingers on the steering wheel and sighed. "I'm going to drive around a little bit before I check in."

"Should you call first and reserve a room?"

"I don't want to give them the chance to turn me away. But I don't want to get there right after Reilly, either. I'll wait a few hours."

"Let me know what happens."

To Rex, Eddie's voice sounded defeated. "Don't worry, Eddie. This time Sunday you'll be Mr. Lucretia Standish."

There was a click in Rex's ear.

"No sense of humor," he muttered as he drove away from the winery.

19

Nora and Luke rode the elevator up to their suite at the Four Seasons Hotel. They had only a half hour to get ready before meeting Wally and Bev for dinner.

"How did I do today?" Nora asked Luke as he held the door open for her. She was referring to her two-line cameo in the television movie of one of her books.

"Brilliant as usual," Luke replied in his deadpan voice. "I'm your biggest fan."

Nora laughed as they walked into the elegant sitting room. Everything was spotless. Nora glanced toward the bedroom off the sitting room. "I'd love to take a nap, but I think we'd better start to get ready," she said, making her way into the large marble bathroom.

With that statement the phone rang. Luke picked it up.

"Hi there, Wally. . . . You'll pick us up? Great. . . . Seven-thirty it is then."

Luke hung up the phone. "We have a little extra time. Wally had a meeting that ran late."

"Perfect. I'll put my robe on and relax."

◆　　◆　　◆

At eight o'clock Nora, Luke, Wally, and Bev were seated in a booth at a quiet Italian restaurant in Beverly Hills.

"I can hear myself think here," Wally said as he snapped his fingers and grabbed a piece of the warm bread.

Bev nodded and sipped her water.

"I'm sorry Regan couldn't be with us," Wally continued. "Nice gal. A nice gal you've got there."

"Yes. Well, she just got back from vacation and got a call about a girl who took off from a movie set she's working on near Santa Barbara."

"What movie?" Wally asked quickly.

"Jinxed."

Wally's eyes opened wide. "I know the director, a youngish kid about thirty. He's pretty good. I was actually thinking of him for one of my projects. I should give him a call." He took out the small black notebook he always carried with him and wrote himself a note.

20

———◆———

I'll make us some dinner," Lilac said when the news was over.
"Regan, you're going to stay with us tonight, aren't you?"

"That would be a good idea," Regan agreed. "After dinner we
can start calling the hotels and motels again."

Leon drained his wineglass. "What are the chances of our
just happening to find Whitney a second time in one day?"

"Better to light a candle than curse the darkness," Earl said
positively. "Regan, why don't I show you to a room right now? Do
you have a bag in the car?"

"Yes."

"How about if we eat in an hour?" Lilac suggested.

"Sounds great," Regan replied.

The bedroom had a simple country charm, much in keeping
with the rest of Altered States. A pine dresser and bed with a
simple white spread and a colorful area rug gave a warm, cheery
feel. A sliding glass door opened onto the backyard with a view
of acres and acres of rolling hills.

"This is lovely," Regan said as Earl put her bag on the bed.

"There's so much more we can do to make Altered States a
first-rate winery, meditation center, and hotel," he said. "It's so
incredibly peaceful here. I'm glad to get out of the rat race."

Rat race, Regan thought. This guy looks as if he's never been in any sort of race in his life. "Oh?" she said innocently. "What did you do?"

"I had a company that dug for oil. I had a partner. Sometimes it worked, sometimes it was a bust. All in all, too much stress. Then I discovered the spiritual life."

Now I've heard everything, Regan thought. This guy certainly doesn't look like your typical oilman.

When Earl left, Regan called Jack. She got his voice mail and left him a message about Edward Fields. She then opened the sliding glass door and walked outside. The air smelled earthy and fresh. There you go, Regan thought. Freshness. Where is she?

Regan brushed her teeth, washed her face, reapplied her makeup, and then changed her outfit. I'm not only looking for Freshness, but I'm striving for freshness, she thought as she headed out to the reception area.

"Come on into the dining room," Lilac greeted Regan. She had set an attractive, inviting table. Candles flickered, reflecting light off the crystal wineglasses. Fresh flowers, not so high that you couldn't see over them, were in a vase in the middle of the table. Soft music was playing on the sound system. There was a feeling of peace and harmony. "My brothers will be out in a minute."

Regan and Lilac both turned simultaneously as they heard an unfamiliar male voice calling from the other room: "Hello?"

A large fellow wearing black jeans and a black leather jacket appeared in the doorway. He had black hair that looked unnatural to Regan, but he seemed genuinely friendly.

"Can I help you?" Lilac asked.

"I hope so. I was wondering if you have any rooms for the night."

"Yes, we do. Let's go to the desk and get you registered."

Now this place has two guests, Regan thought. If Jack were here, it would be three. Oh, well. No such luck. It seemed to Regan that Lilac was not thrilled to have another guest. She realized that Lilac wanted to focus on finding Whitney. Heck, that would be worth a lot more than the profit from a guest for one night. I wonder if Lilac has to provide him with dinner.

When they returned to the dining room, Lilac introduced Don Lesser to Regan, and even though she didn't have to, she offered him dinner. He accepted but insisted on sitting at his own table. "I don't want to disturb you. I'll just have a glass of wine and some bread and whatever you're having, and I'll read my book."

He sat across the room, but it was so quiet that Regan knew he could hear everything they were saying. That's the awkward thing about sitting next to a lone diner in any restaurant. You know he has nothing better to do than eavesdrop.

Leon was particularly morose. "What are you going to do if we don't find Whitney at any of the hotels we call tonight?" he asked Regan.

"I was thinking of driving back down to the hotel where the movie is based. I can't believe that somebody there doesn't have some information on where she might be."

"That's logical," Earl said as he ate a forkful of whole wheat pasta with tomato sauce.

Lilac had made a salad, heated Italian bread, and whipped up a delicious sauce made from what Regan was sure were organic products. Regan twirled several strands of pasta onto her fork but dropped her utensil when Lilac let out a high-pitched scream.

"What?" Regan cried.

"Freshness!" Lilac jumped up and went running over to her daughter, who was standing in the doorway.

To Regan it was as if they all had seen a ghost.

"Mom!" Freshness/Whitney laughed. "I've never had such an enthusiastic greeting from you."

It also seemed to Regan like one of those moments on a game show when the contestant wins the big money. The contestant usually loses nearly all control, depending on the size of the jackpot. And Lilac and her brothers had just won a big jackpot. Leon jumped out of his seat, knocking over the wine bottle, and even Earl abandoned his cool and calm demeanor. They both raced over to embrace their niece.

"What is going on?" Whitney asked, nodding hello to the man sitting by himself who was watching her with what Regan thought was great intensity. Well, Whitney was a very attractive girl and obviously provoked quite a reaction from her relatives.

"You're not going to believe it!" Lilac began, leading her daughter to the table.

Another chair was quickly pulled up, Regan was introduced, and Lilac related the story of Lucretia's wedding to Whitney. She lowered her voice, but not when she spoke of the $2 million check that awaited each family member if the whole group showed up.

"Two million dollars!" Whitney cried. "To think I almost didn't come home. Who is she marrying?"

"A con artist. I just know it," Leon said. "But if we each get two million dollars, I'll be happy. Regan, you should look into that guy. But first I'd like to make a toast . . . to my beautiful niece. Thank God you came home. And to Uncle Haskell, may you rest in peace. We're finally getting your money."

They all laughed and drank and toasted their good fortune. Regan could see how happy Whitney was with her mother and uncles. She was a cute girl, and thank God she'd made it home. Now everyone could be happy.

"I have to be at a seminar tomorrow morning," Whitney said as she drained her wineglass.

"What?" her mother asked abruptly.

"It's a one-day acting seminar not too far from here. It ends early Sunday morning. I'll meet you at Lucretia's at noon."

"I'm afraid to let you out of our sight," Leon exclaimed, putting his hand around her forearm.

"Oh, Leon, I'll be fine," Whitney assured her uncle. "Don't you think I could use the money, too? And I can't wait to meet Lucretia. I'd love to talk to her about her acting days."

"From what we saw of her on television, she's still a character," Lilac said.

Regan watched this unusual family and was happy for them that they'd be able to keep the winery/meditation center/bed-and-breakfast going with the money they'd receive on Sunday. But my work is over, she thought. I'll spend the night and go home in the morning.

Of course it wouldn't turn out that way.

Across the room, Rex couldn't believe his ears. They're each going to get 2 million bucks for showing up at the wedding! That idiot Eddie hadn't mentioned that. He guessed it didn't matter, because they weren't going to collect that money. Whitney was sitting across the room from him. It was his job to make sure she didn't get anywhere near the wedding on Sunday. He couldn't believe his good luck once again! Now he just had to get rid of Whitney for the next forty-eight hours—until Edward and Lucretia had safely said "I do" and before anyone like Whitney would be urged to "speak now or forever hold your peace."

She'll hold her peace, Eddie, Rex thought. I'll make sure of it.

He took a sip of his wine and occasionally stole a glance at the group as they laughed and talked. They won't be so chipper on Sunday, he thought, because Whitney is going to disappear again. And he had a feeling that this time it might have to be for good.

21

After dinner, Regan and the family moved to the main room by the reception desk where comfortable couches and armchairs surrounded a huge stone fireplace. Lilac served fruit and coffee, and Regan learned more about the Weldons.

Lilac and Leon were both divorced, and Earl had never married. Their parents had died in the last five years. Whitney was the only child of her generation.

"I can't believe you were actually at the movie set today, Regan," Whitney marveled.

"We were intent on finding you, dear," Lilac said.

Leon tapped his forehead. "And to think we called the motel and you had just left."

Whitney laughed. "I have to get my credit card back."

Don Lesser had gone outside for a walk to get some night air. He was gone for about an hour and then came back in and retreated to his room.

"I'd better get to bed, too," Whitney said with a yawn. "I'm getting up early."

"Keep your cell phone on this weekend," Leon urged her. "Please! Go with the flow almost cost us eight million dollars!"

Even Earl agreed that maybe go-with-the-flow weekends

should be a thing of the past. They were all convivial at the thought of their banking day on Monday.

"Don't worry!" Whitney said. "I don't ever want to be out of touch again. And Mom, I just realized I don't have anything with me that I can wear on Sunday."

"Come look in my closet," Lilac suggested. "There must be something you can wear."

Regan said her good-nights and went to her room. She had never had such an easy case. Get hired to look for a girl, and the girl shows up at home. Not bad. Well, she thought, I'll get a good night's sleep, head home tomorrow morning, and have the weekend to get organized. She sat down on the bed and pulled out her cell phone. She had turned off the phone when they were having dinner. The second little envelope on the screen indicated that she had a message—it was from Jack.

"Hey, Regan. I hope it's going well. I have a little information about Lucretia. As you know she made a fortune from one of the dot-coms that went bust. And as for the guy she's marrying, I'm checking around, but I don't have much to go on. I'm going home now to go to sleep. If you want to leave a message on my cell phone, please call. I'll get it when I wake up in the morning. I miss you. Good night, sweetie."

Regan grinned. She called him back and said, "My case is over. Whitney walked into Altered States tonight. You should have seen the look on her mother's face. Anyway, I'm heading home tomorrow. As for the groom-to-be, I don't know much about him. I think I'll get Whitney's mother to call the bride to-morrow. Maybe she can get some information about Lucretia's fiancé. He does seem suspicious. On the news report tonight he definitely hid from the cameras. I miss you, too."

Regan opened the sliding glass door to get some air. There was a safety bolt on the screen that made it feel safe to leave the door open while she slept. After washing her face and brushing her teeth, Regan was thrilled to get into the comfortable bed. It had been a long day. She fell into a deep sleep almost as soon as her head hit the pillow.

Regan woke up a couple of times during the night. Once at 4:00 A.M. she thought she heard footsteps in the hallway. Then at 5:30 she awoke with a start. This time there was a strange sound upstairs where the family's bedrooms were. She waited. It was all calm and quiet. She could hear a very slight rustling of the wind through the screen door. Whitney is probably getting ready to leave, Regan realized. She said she wanted to be on the road by six. Regan rolled over and went back to sleep.

Saturday, May 11

22

———◆———

Whitney had hardly slept. She couldn't believe that she'd have the money to give to Frank to finish the movie. But she didn't want to call him about it until she had the check in hand. If it didn't happen, she couldn't bear the thought of his disappointment.

At five o'clock she got out of bed, wrapped herself in a robe, and went down the hall to shower. Twenty minutes later she was dressed and ready to go. The dress her mother had given her to wear to the wedding was on a hanger in the closet, covered with plastic from the dry cleaner's. She grabbed the dress, along with her bag, and tiptoed downstairs. She didn't bother to make coffee. She'd pick some up at the diner on the road. They made great java and opened at dawn.

The lodge was still. Everyone else was asleep. She smiled, looking forward to everything that was about to change in their lives. No more money worries about this place. If the movie was a success, she didn't even dare to contemplate what that meant to Frank and her. With plenty of money left over, she wouldn't have to juggle credit cards!

Outside, her car was parked under one of the large oak trees that seemed to filter out any light, no matter the time of day.

The dark blue sky was just starting to surrender to the effects of the rising sun. It's such an interesting time of day to be awake, she thought as an occasional chirp from a bird broke the silence. But it does feel a little eerie.

She walked across the driveway to her Jeep, opened the door, and threw her bag onto the passenger seat. She leaned in and knelt on the driver's seat, poised to hang her dress on the hook above the window in the back.

"Huhhh," she cried, inhaling sharply. The king-sized quilt she kept in the back for when she went to the beach was, as usual, rumpled on the floor. But even in the gray light of early morning, she could see that something was different. There was something under it that had not been there last night. She started to move backward off the seat when the quilt loomed up and a hand reached from under it and grabbed her.

"Stay," the voice commanded in a harsh tone. "Close the door. And don't try anything. I have a gun."

Whitney's head started to spin. Tears stung her eyes. Her family was sleeping peacefully such a short distance away. They had no idea she was in trouble, and when they found out, it would be too late.

"Move it," the male voice said again as he pulled her right arm roughly.

Keep your cool, she thought. The dress on the hanger was still in her left hand. Whoever was under the quilt couldn't see it, she was sure. She slid into the driver's seat and let the dress and hanger slide down onto the ground outside. She shut the door and started the car. She could feel the quilt brushing against her shoulder and neck.

"Go out the driveway nice and slowly. Then you're going to take the dirt road off the main drag that leads to that old barn. You know the one I mean, don't you?"

"Yes," Whitney answered as calmly as she could. It was the barn that housed a bunch of rusty old equipment from years back. Leon planned to clean it out and restore it when he got his $2 million. Nobody went back there now. They had talked about it last night.

"That's good, because that's where we're going."

Is he going to kill me? Whitney wondered frantically as she drove. Does he really have a gun? Her brain told her to do what he said as her heart pounded wildly. But who was he? And what did he want from her? I'll know soon enough, she thought as she bit her lip, passing the Altered States Winery sign, the sign that had made her feel so welcome just last night.

23

At 8:15 Regan joined Lilac and Earl for breakfast at the table where they'd dined the night before.

"I suppose Whitney got off this morning," Regan remarked as Lilac poured her a cup of coffee.

"Her room is empty. I'm sure she's at the seminar by now."

Leon walked in, carrying a dress covered with plastic. "This was on the ground outside."

Lilac looked up. "That's the dress I lent to Whitney for the wedding. Where was it?"

"Right next to where her car was parked."

Regan didn't like the apprehensive feeling that came over her. She knew Whitney didn't have much baggage. How could she have dropped the dress and not notice it?

"That's our Whitney," Earl said as he peeled a banana and began to slice it over his cereal bowl.

None of them seem concerned, Regan thought.

"I'll call her to let her know we have it," Lilac said simply.

Leon looked tired. He took the chair next to Regan and rubbed his eyes. "There are wildfires out there that are headed this way."

"You're kidding!" Lilac said. "Since when?"

"I just heard it on the news. Kids were smoking behind a school last night. One cigarette started the fire. They've been working all night to contain it, but the wind keeps switching directions so the fire is spreading."

Regan knew how dangerous wildfires could be. One day you have acres of vineyards, and the next they're charred ruins. She doubted that Leon would leave for a wedding if his land was in danger.

Leon had put the dress over the back of a chair at the next table. The sight of the dress made Regan uneasy. It just doesn't make sense, she thought. I don't think I should leave here just yet.

"Earl," Regan said. "Do you mind if I join your meditation class this morning?"

"Ten A.M. in the barn. Wear loose clothing."

"Stay and relax, Regan," Lilac said, smiling. "It's a beautiful day. You don't have to get back right away, do you?"

"No," Regan answered honestly. She didn't want to share her concerns with Lilac, but she didn't want to leave until she knew that Whitney was okay. Regan had one of those gut feelings. "Are you going to call Lucretia?" Regan asked. "Maybe we can find out more about the fiancé."

"Good idea," Lilac said. "But not this early. I will call Freshness, though."

"If she's in her seminar, she won't answer," Earl informed them. "I know those seminars. Cell phones are forbidden."

"I'll leave her a message then."

"Lilac," Regan said. "I'd like to be there when you talk to Lucretia. Can we call her from your office?"

"Sounds good."

Regan slathered raspberry jam on a corn muffin and bit into it. It was delicious. As a bed-and-breakfast this place definitely worked. The lodge had charm and warmth, and the accommodations and food were more than satisfactory. The winery was making progress, and they'd won a medal for their pinot noir. The tasting room would certainly attract people for years to come. Earl and his meditation center—who knows?

Lilac, Earl, and Leon were all doing what they loved to do. They wanted to eventually buy more land and plant more vineyards. Not bad work if you can get it, Regan thought.

When she had finished breakfast, Regan excused herself and went back to her room. It would be so nice if Jack were here, she thought as she dialed his number. When he answered, she recounted everything that had happened.

"I don't like the sound of it, either," Jack mused. "I wonder how many people know about the money the family is supposed to get."

"They say they haven't told anyone."

"Lucretia is all over the news, you know."

"She is?" Regan asked, surprised.

"That piece on her wedding and the fact that she is bragging about having made so much money on a dot-com makes for a good human interest story. Life begins at ninety-three. They keep replaying the interview over and over."

"Oh my God," Regan said.

"It's obvious Lucretia loves the limelight. The same can't be said about her intended. I'm having a couple of guys out in the L.A. office see what they can find out about him."

"Thanks, Jack."

"I'll keep you posted," he promised.

As soon as Regan hung up, her cell phone rang.

"Hi, honey," her mother said when Regan answered.

"Hi, Mom. What's going on?"

"Well, your father and I have nothing to do until tomorrow afternoon. We'd love to see you."

A thought occurred to Regan. Well, why not? she wondered. These people could use the business. "How about spending the night at a winery?" Regan asked. "It's beautiful up here, and they have rooms." She explained to Nora everything that had been going on. "And it's only a couple of hours' drive."

"That sounds great," Nora said after consulting with Luke. "We'll be there in time to go out to lunch."

24

At first Lucretia was thrilled with all the attention the national news channel stirred up. The phone started ringing Friday evening with calls from people she didn't even know were still alive. Others claimed they didn't know she was still alive. Childhood chums who were still hanging in there called to say hello. Friends of her past husbands called. People she'd met on cruise ships called. They were all invited to the wedding. Some who lived close enough actually accepted the invitation.

Then in the middle of the night the threatening calls started.

"You stole that money from me!" one voice cried into the phone at four o'clock in the morning. "I'm going to make you pay for that."

"Your boyfriend is a jerk. Don't marry him," warned another.

And, worse yet, someone called to say that she'd seen Lucretia's films and thought she was a lousy actress. That bugged her more than anything. She could barely sleep. At six o'clock she walked out to get the paper and found smashed tomatoes all over her beautiful front steps.

"You're supposed to throw rice when someone gets married," she mumbled to herself. She thought of calling Edward, but she knew how he loved his rest. He could be so boring at times. I definitely wouldn't be marrying him if I were fifty years younger, she thought. She even felt a little guilty about it.

Lucretia gathered up the paper, which must have arrived after the tomatoes because it was unblemished, and went inside. She went back to her room and finally managed to doze off, waking only when she heard Phyllis's car in the driveway.

Phyllis reached the front steps and scowled as only Phyllis could. "What the heck?" she grumbled as she unlocked the door and stepped inside.

In the kitchen she put on the coffeepot and waited for the buzz from Lucretia. Lucretia did not disappoint.

Phyllis poured the coffee and brought it into Lucretia's bedroom.

"My last day as a single woman," Lucretia proclaimed as she propped herself up on the pillows.

Give me a break, Phyllis thought.

"And this is going to be my last wedding!"

"You never know," Phyllis said as she placed the breakfast tray in front of her boss.

"Phyllis, sit down. I had a terrible night."

"I saw the tomatoes outside."

"Who would do such a thing?"

"I can't imagine."

"I'm an old lady who wants a little happiness."

"You're a rich old lady who wants a little happiness," Phyllis corrected her. "That makes a big difference to some people, especially people who maybe lost money in the stock market or the dot-coms. That television piece might have stirred something up in them, like bitterness or resentment or anger or envy."

Lucretia thought about this for a moment as she sipped her coffee. "They could be jealous I'm marrying Edward."

Phyllis managed a shrug.

"Are we all set for tomorrow?" Lucretia asked.

"Yes. Everything's done. You just have to give the caterer a final number after you stop inviting people."

"Phyllis, that's half the fun."

The phone next to the bed rang. They both eyed it. Phyllis picked it up. "Standish residence." She listened, then yelled into the receiver, "You're very rude!"

"Who was that?" Lucretia asked.

"Wrong number."

"No, it wasn't!" Lucretia cried. "This is supposed to be a happy time for me. Now I don't want to be in my own home. I don't want to hear the phone ring again."

It rang as if on cue.

Phyllis picked it up again. "Standish residence. . . . Oh, Lucretia's niece," Phyllis almost stammered. "Of course. Lucretia's right here."

"Lilac!" Lucretia yelped into the phone. It was as though she were just thrown a life preserver. "I do hope you're coming tomorrow."

I'm sure she is, Phyllis thought smugly.

"How wonderful. I can't wait to meet you. . . . You saw the piece on TV. . . . Well, I guess it upset some people." Lucretia explained in dramatic fashion the phone calls and the mess on her front steps. "There's tomato sauce all over the place," she cried. "I'm scared to be here, honestly. I'm shaking all over."

Boy, does she play for sympathy, Phyllis thought. But Lucretia's next sentence almost sent her over the edge.

"Come up there today?" Lucretia said, a smile forming on her lips. "Meditation . . . a nice dinner . . . family time . . . drive down in the morning. That sounds like the perfect solution. Everything here is done, and I have all day to be nervous."

Phyllis interrupted her: "Don't you think you need your rest today?"

Lucretia shushed her. "No!" she hissed, then turned back to the phone. "Nothing, Lilac darling. Everything's fine. I'll call Edward and tell him this is the plan for today. Of course he'll want to come! I haven't been to a winery in years. It'll be fabulous. A ride in the country always did me good." She wrote down the directions and told Lilac she'd see her that afternoon.

They'd better not double-cross me, Phyllis thought frantically. "Can I come with you?" she blurted out.

Lucretia looked at her as though she were nuts. "Since when did you want to travel with me? Besides, this is my pre-honeymoon. Also, you have to stick around here to answer the doorbell. The caterer and the florist will be making deliveries today."

Phyllis knew she was right. But she was terrified that somehow her deal with Lilac would fall through. Everything suddenly felt out of her control.

"I must call Edward," Lucretia cried. "Now get out my overnight bag."

25

Rex was back in bed. He couldn't believe that he had pulled it off. Whitney was in the barn where no one could possibly find her—at least not for a long while. She was tucked away safe and sound until after the wedding. Rex had managed to sneak back into the house undetected. That was over two hours ago.

He got up, grabbed his cell phone, went into the bathroom, turned on the shower, and dialed Eddie's number. A groggy-sounding Eddie answered.

"It's me," Rex announced.

"What's going on, man?" Eddie asked.

"I got her. She's tied up in the garage."

"Are you kidding?" Eddie's voice went up an octave. "Is she safe?"

"Safe enough. I'm trying to decide what to do now."

"What do you mean?"

"Should I stay here or should I leave?"

"Stay. Make sure Whitney stays put in the garage. Where's Regan Reilly?"

"Still here, I suppose. I'm in my room."

"Stay. Keep an eye on things."

"Okay. What's going on down there?"

"It's a nightmare. We were on the news last night. Lucretia's announcing our marriage to the world. I'm a wreck."

"You were on the news? How did that happen?"

"She shopped for a wedding dress at Saks and started yakking away with the salesgirl. One thing led to another."

"Nobody said marrying someone worth over fifty million dollars would be easy. By the way, did you know that Whitney and her family are all getting a couple of million dollars each if the group shows up at the wedding?"

"What? How do they know that? Lucretia told me to make out the checks, but it was supposed to be a surprise." He paused. "And they're getting it whether they show up at the wedding or not. Why would they think it has to do with showing up? I wonder if that nosy maid has anything to do with it. Now it makes sense that they hired a private investigator to find Whitney! They're doing it because they think they'll get money. How greedy."

"Well, my friend, they think the same of you. They suspect you're a con artist. They're right about that."

Eddie's call waiting clicked in his ear. "Hold on a second," he said.

Rex waited, sitting on the edge of the bathtub. A couple of minutes ticked by. He got up and looked at himself in the mirror. I hate wearing the dopey wig, he thought. He was contemplating that maybe he could use some surgery to get rid of the bags under his eyes when Eddie came back on the line.

"Oh my God!" Eddie cried.

"What's the matter?" Rex asked quickly. He'd never heard Eddie sound so distressed.

"Lucretia had a bad night. Then she talked to Whitney's mother. We're invited up there today to relax, have a nice dinner, and stay over. We'll come back for the wedding in the morning."

Rex whistled softly. "Oh, boy. Can't you get out if it?"

"No. There's a tone in Lucretia's voice that I haven't heard before. She's determined."

"Well, pal, I guess I'll be seeing you later today. Remember, we don't know each other." Rex hung up the phone. Maybe I shouldn't stay, he thought. This may be getting a little too close for comfort. As long as Whitney was hidden, Rex didn't have anything to do. He called another one of his cohorts in New York to check up on another "project." The news wasn't good.

"Jimmy got arrested when he tried to sell the artwork to an undercover officer. The feds are questioning him."

Oh, great, Rex thought. I guess I'm not going anywhere. It's time to lay low at the winery. Time to just lay low. Maybe I'll take the meditation class.

26

Frank Kipsman woke up with a headache. He knew it was tension. He'd driven down to the Beverly Hills Hotel last night with Heidi Durst, the screenwriter and producer of *Jinxed*. Heidi was a nightmare. It was bad enough that she created tension on the set for the actors, but she ranted and raved for the entire ride, going on about how *Jinxed* has to work and how they should have done this and should have done that. They both knew the financial difficulties were her fault, but Frank knew he had to let her vent. Her backers had pulled out because she had been so difficult to deal with.

God, how he missed Whitney. Sweet, ditzy Whitney. How lucky he was that she auditioned for *Jinxed*. She was perfect. A young Goldie Hawn. She played the part of the beleaguered dot-com executive with perfect aplomb, as they say. This movie could really advance her career. His, too.

Frank switched on the bedside light and called the beeper he had given Whitney. He knew that she didn't want to keep checking her cell phone. The beeper was a quicker and easier way to stay in touch because it was just for the two of them. No one else had the number. They laughed about it being romantic. All Whitney had to do was look at the number, confirm it was

Frank's, and call back as soon as she could. He dialed the number of the beeper, plugged in his number, hung up his phone, and waited.

For ten minutes he lay on the bed. He looked at his watch. It was 8:15. He told her he'd call her early in the morning. Where could she be? he wondered as he started to feel uneasy.

Twenty-eight years old, the boyish Frank had already established a name for himself as an up-and-comer in Hollywood. He'd made a couple of low-budget slasher movies, and *Jinxed* was his first chance at a comedy. *The Three Stooges* had been his favorite show when he was a kid and inspired him to get into show biz. He knew *Jinxed* could be a big hit, and that was why he could put up with the supreme taskmaster, Heidi Durst. She was demanding and egocentric, and put everyone around her through a wringer, but she was also a talented producer. And she could be very funny, even if it was mostly in a mean way.

What made him feel really uncomfortable was that he thought she had a crush on him. It was unrequited love as not even Shakespeare could imagine. Heidi was only thirty-one, but she was as crusty as any curmudgeon coming down the pike. Bitter about having lost a husband to someone who was actually a nice person, Heidi put all her hopes into this movie.

Frank got up and opened the curtains to another bright, sunny day in Los Angeles. He was supposed to meet Heidi downstairs in the Polo Lounge for breakfast at a quarter to nine. I can't wait to hear her new scheme, he thought as he headed for the shower. We come down here for the weekend to raise a million dollars without any real plan, and we stay in an expensive hotel to try to impress potential backers.

Fifteen minutes later, dressed in chinos, a navy blazer, and his trademark sneakers, Frank joined Heidi in the restaurant. She was already seated, making notes on her legal pad, swigging coffee, and barking orders at the waiter. Here we go, Frank thought as he took in the sight of her. It's not that Heidi was unattractive; it was her demeanor that made people run for cover. Curly brown hair that was clipped by what looked like a military barber, intense blue eyes, and a determined jaw said it all. She had on a khaki pantsuit that made her look as if she were going into battle. Well, I guess she is, Frank thought as he smiled and took the seat opposite her.

"Morning, Kipsman," she said brusquely.

"Good morning." He unfolded the napkin and put it across his lap, well aware that it was going to be a long day. And all he wanted to do was make movies.

Heidi looked down at her legal pad. "My assistant called this morning. Several people we contacted have agreed to see us today. But I have another idea."

"What's that?" Frank asked as he gratefully accepted coffee from the waiter.

"I couldn't sleep last night, so I was watching GOS. They kept playing this brief piece about a woman who's getting married this weekend. She made over fifty million in one of the dotcoms that crashed."

Frank just nodded.

"She's ninety-three."

Frank nodded again.

"She's marrying a much younger man."

"Uh-huh."

"She used to be a silent film star."

"Oh, really."

"Yes, really," Heidi repeated, sounding annoyed. "She was very big for about five minutes—seventy-five years ago."

Frank hadn't seen many silent films. He'd been too busy watching the Three Stooges.

"She lives in Beverly Hills. I checked. Her phone number is in the book. I'm going to call her and offer her a part in the movie."

"Offer her a part in the movie?" Frank gulped.

"Yes! We'll figure out something. She can play herself—someone who made a fortune off a dot-com instead of losing everything. It can be a brief scene over the closing credits. It'll be funny and good for publicity."

"I assume you'll be seeking funds from her."

"Well, what do you think?" Heidi snapped. "I'm going to call her this morning and tell her we have a wedding present that we'd love to drop off since we're in town—"

"Do you have a present?" Frank asked.

"Of course not. We'll go shopping if she agrees to see us."

Frank sipped his coffee. Why oh why hadn't Whitney called back?

27

Frank and Heidi had a most unsuccessful meeting with a potential investor who told them their movie would never work. Frank had the feeling that the guy just wanted to sit and talk about the lousy movies he had made years ago. They sat in his den as he smoked a pipe and went on and on about this actor and that actor. He seemed to start every sentence with "In my day . . ."

When it became clear that the checkbook on his desk would not be opened for *Jinxed* anytime in this millennium, they extricated themselves as quickly as possible. They were down but not out.

"We have to meet the next moneybags in half an hour, but let's see if I can reach Lucretia Standish," Heidi said as she dialed her cell phone. She cleared her throat and waited. Frank knew the look. She was like a tiger, poised to spring on her unsuspecting prey.

"Is Miss Lucretia Standish there?" she asked in her friendliest tone.

Frank sat back and folded his arms. He still couldn't believe Whitney hadn't called back. But he couldn't say a word to Heidi. She'd freak if she knew there was anything going on between them. She'd already said a few snide things about Whitney. Heidi knew she was talented, so she had no reason to complain. She was just jealous because everyone liked Whitney.

To be your own man, Frank thought. Well, I guess everybody has to kiss somebody's behind no matter where you are on the food chain.

"This is Heidi Durst, president of Gold Rush films. . . . No, I don't know Ms. Standish. . . . Well, I have what I think will be good news for her. We know that she's an actress, and we wanted to offer her a part in the movie we're currently filming. . . . Yes, now. . . . Of course I'll hold." Heidi turned and looked triumphantly at Frank. "The maid is running after her. She's out in the car. What people will do when Hollywood calls. It's pathetic," she said with superiority.

Her superiority was short-lived.

"Miss Standish, helllloooo," she said. "Yes, that is right. We would love to work with you, and we thought we might stop by your house today. . . . Not good, huh? . . ."

Frank wasn't the least bit surprised.

"Oh, I see. . . . You're heading up to your niece and nephews' winery. . . . Tomorrow's the wedding, and you'll be away for a couple of weeks. . . . Well, our movie doesn't finish shooting for another month, so we could still use you. If you have a minute, we're right in the neighborhood."

Frank thought the voice at the other end of the phone sounded like Cousin Itt from *The Addams Family*. That was another one of his favorite shows even though it was produced long before he was born. Thank God for cable.

"We could have a glass of wine with you at the winery later today. . . . That sounds wonderful. . . . We're heading up that way anyhow." Heidi wrote down the directions. "The Altered States Winery . . ."

JINXED

⸺◆⸺

Frank inhaled sharply, causing Heidi to look at him quizzically. He smiled back as though everything was fine—everything except that that was Whitney's family's business.

How much did they know about him?

28

At Norman Broda's acting seminar, he took attendance, which didn't take long at all. There were eleven students who would be spending the day learning how to release their creativity, remove blocks, unleash their own voice, their own self. "Mine the vein of gold that is you" was Norman's battle cry.

A day and a night of this with a dozen students added up to six grand. Not bad if you do it a couple of times a month.

Norman was most disappointed that Whitney Weldon hadn't shown up yet. As it was they were getting a late start, and she still wasn't here. He wondered where she could be. She'd already ponied up the $500. And that was just yesterday. It was unusual for someone to sign up so late and then not attend the seminar.

Norman had been hoping to use Whitney's name to attract more attendees at these seminars. He was considered a wizard at getting actors to loosen up. He had taught in Hollywood and then retreated to the mountains three years ago to write screenplays. Two had actually been optioned. He still directed an occasional television movie. All in all it was a good life. Age fifty-two, he lived with his girlfriend, Dew, who was twenty-five and worked at the radio station in town.

He had the feeling that he should call Whitney to see if she was coming. He normally didn't do that. If someone didn't show up, she didn't show up. But he had actually answered the phone yesterday when Whitney called, and she sounded so excited about the seminar.

No, he decided. I'll wait until lunchtime. If she isn't here, then I'll call. If I can't reach her, I'll call Ricky and find out what happened. Maybe she can come to the next seminar in a couple of weeks. He'd love to get her to read the script he had just written. She would be perfect for the lead.

"Okay, everyone," he said to the students. "I want you all to bring a chair up onstage. . . . We're going to start with sense memory exercises."

As he led the group through an introductory relaxation technique, he couldn't get his mind off Whitney Weldon.

Where was she?

29

Whitney was a prisoner in her own car. Her hands and feet were bound, her eyes were blindfolded, and a gag was tied around her mouth. The car was hidden in the back of the barn where no one would ever find it until they decided to clear out the place. The building was full of junk: old tractors, oak barrels, falling-apart furniture. Whitney thought she'd heard her captor throwing things over the car. Clearly he had been here earlier.

He had thrown the quilt over her as soon as she stopped the car. In that quick moment she had seen in the rearview mirror that he was wearing a ski mask. He'd shoved her roughly to the storage area behind the backseat and then tied her up.

When will anyone miss me? she wondered. Her family had begged her to keep her cell phone on and to be sure to keep in touch. The wedding tomorrow was too important to miss.

Whitney lay there with her hands tied behind her back. The gag in her mouth tightened when she tried to scream, as if it would choke her if she tried too hard. The blindfold was so tight around her eyes that her head throbbed. What can I hope for? she wondered. Will someone find me? Will I be left here to die?

Maybe, just maybe, they'll miss me at the seminar. Maybe they'll call to see where I am. It was her only hope.

30

After Regan hung up with her parents, she still couldn't shake the feeling of concern for Whitney. It just didn't make sense that Whitney would drop her dress and not notice it, no matter how rushed she felt and no matter how early in the day it was.

But what could have happened?

Regan walked out of her room, down the hallway, and into the grand room of the lodge. All was quiet. She glanced out a front window and saw three women getting out of their cars, dressed as if they were going to join Earl's meditation class. It was a beautiful May morning. The sun was shining, and it was one of those days when everything should come up roses.

In the office Regan found Lilac conversing with a woman who was probably in her forties and was dressed in jeans and a floral sweater.

"Regan, this is Bella. She helps us with everything around here."

"Oh, I just love every minute of it," Bella said as she grabbed Regan's hand, squeezed the life out of it, and pumped it several times. "How are you, Regan?" she asked. Her body was broad, but her face looked like a Kewpie doll's, with dramatic carefully lined red lips. They reminded Regan of a bow tie. Brown hair curled around her lined face.

Regan pulled her hand back, resisting the urge to massage it, and replied, "Nice to meet you, too, Bella."

Bella turned her attention back to Lilac. "I'll go open the candle shop. We're also open all day for tastings?"

"Sip, sip, sip," Lilac chirped. "I'll be over in a few minutes."

When Bella left, Lilac said, "Regan, you still haven't had the tour. The tasting room and the candle shop are in a little building next to the meditation center."

"I'd like to see it all," Regan said. "How long has Bella worked for you?"

"She just started this week."

"She did?" Regan was surprised to hear the surprise in her voice.

"She pulled up the driveway, got out, and started chatting up a storm. She just moved down from Washington State a few weeks ago with her husband. He got a new job around here. It turns out that her grandfather owned this place when it went bust because of Prohibition. She'd never been here and wanted to see it for herself. We got to talking, and the next thing you know I hired her."

"Wow," Regan said. "What does her husband do?"

"He works in the pub downtown."

Regan raised her eyebrows. "So they've got beer and wine covered."

"I guess so," Lilac said, laughing. "I called Lucretia."

"Already?"

"Yes. First I called Whitney and left a message on her cell phone, then I dialed Lucretia."

Thanks, Regan thought. Lilac is a ditz, too. She had obviously forgotten her promise to have Regan with her when she made that call.

"She's coming up here today with her fiancé."

"You're kidding!" Regan wondered what other surprises Lilac had in store for her as she listened to the story of Lucretia's bad night.

"Well, this should be interesting," Regan noted when Lilac finished. "I just spoke to my parents, and they'd like to come up and spend the night."

"Wonderful! We'll have a big dinner."

"That sounds terrific," Regan enthused. "We can check out Lucretia's fiancé in the flesh." She then put her hands together in front of her face, hesitating slightly. "Lilac, I'd really like to try and reach Whitney at the acting workshop."

"Why?"

"I guess I'm a worrier. I'd just like to know that she got there safely."

Lilac smiled. "You don't know our Whitney. When she was little, I used to have to pull her head out of the cereal bowl in the morning. She doesn't wake up easily. I'm sure she doesn't even know the dress is missing." Lilac turned and pulled a number off a bulletin board on the wall. "She did give me the number there. We may as well call."

"I'll do it," Regan offered. She took the piece of paper, picked up the phone on the desk, and dialed. The woman who answered the phone didn't speak English very well. Regan had a hard time communicating with her.

"I tell Mr. Norman to call you later," the woman said. "He busy out in his barn with students. They all screaming and yelling. Sounds crazy."

"If you could see that he gets the message, it would be great," Regan said, praying that this woman would pass it along. Somehow she doubted it. They could always call back later.

When Regan hung up, she looked at Lilac. "I'm now about to take my first meditation class."

"Earl is such an amazing instructor," Lilac assured her. "You are going to feel so relaxed and stress free."

We'll see, Regan thought as she headed out the door.

31

Early Saturday morning the reporter covering Lucretia's impending wedding received a call at home in Los Angeles. Lynne B. Harrison was asleep and reached groggily for the phone.

"Lynne, get up," her boss yelled at her. "You've got to do more on that old lady with all the money who's getting married. We're getting hundreds of phone calls and e-mails."

Lynne blinked and looked at the clock. It wasn't even nine o'clock in the morning, and Saturday was her day off. She'd been out late last night and didn't expect to waken until at least noon.

"What do you want me to do?" she whined.

"Figure out something. This story has captured people's imagination. The idea that you can find love and big money at such an advanced age has everybody interested. Didn't she invite you to the wedding?"

"Yes."

"You're going." It wasn't a question.

"I told her I would. But that's tomorrow."

"Well, you've got to go out there today and get some more footage. I'll have a cameraman at your place in half an hour. We have Lucretia's address. Go to her house and get more background for the story. Find another angle . . . whatever. As you know, May is sweeps month. We've got to pull up our ratings. And May is the month a lot of people get married. Lucretia Standish is inspiring people to just go for it before it's too late. We have to be there to cover it!"

Lynne sat up in bed. Her boss, Alan Wakeman, could certainly be pushy. He was young and trying to make a name for himself in the business. If he thought a story had "legs," he ran it into the ground—or had her run it into the ground.

"Okay, Alan. I'll be ready in half an hour."

32

Lucretia's Rolls-Royce traveled north on Highway 101 with Edward at the wheel and Lucretia sitting shotgun.

"I can't believe you've never been married, darling," Lucretia exclaimed.

Edward turned and glanced down at her. "I was waiting to meet the right woman."

Lucretia giggled. "Why does that line sound rehearsed to me?"

"It's not," Edward protested. "Lucretia, you know there's no one better for me than you. No one more fun than you."

"That's true. All my husbands said I was loads of fun."

Edward felt as if he was driving himself to his own execution. Here he was, on a gorgeous spring day, driving a Rolls-Royce and heading up to a winery, meditation center, and who knows what. And he would rather be almost anywhere else in the world. That stupid television story. If he could just pull off the marriage ceremony, then everything would be fine. The thought of Whitney on the very same property where they were headed made him crazy, even if she was bound and gagged and hidden away.

"I have a great idea," he announced.

"What, darling?"

"Why don't we drive to Las Vegas? We can get married there. We'll get away from the prying eyes of the world. We'll get away from those tomato throwers and all those other nasty people who don't want to see us happy."

Lucretia actually looked as if she might consider his proposal. She blinked several times. "That would be too lonely."

Lonely? Edward wanted to scream. Instead he said, "But we'd be together. And that's all that counts."

Lucretia smiled at him. "We have the rest of our lives to be together. I want my family at the wedding."

"Of course," he said as he snapped on the radio.

"A wildfire is spreading in the area northeast of Santa Barbara. Firefighters have not been able to get it under control."

"That's where we're going." Lucretia sounded alarmed. "I hope it doesn't hit their property, the poor darlings."

Oh my God, Edward thought. Whitney is in an abandoned building. How close is the fire? Would Rex leave her there if the fire became life threatening?

Yes, he would.

Edward stepped on the gas as a car full of teenage girls drove by, obviously recognized them, and started honking the horn. The driver rolled down her window, stuck out her hand, and gave them the thumbs-up sign.

"Congratulations!" she cried.

It took about two seconds for Lucretia to stick her head out the window and wave back. One of the girls took a picture.

Lucretia laughed gaily as she pulled herself inside, sat back, and smoothed her hair. "Those girls remind me of the fun I had when I was young, before I went to Hollywood. My two best friends and I were inseparable. We used to love to go over to the graveyard at night and sit around and talk, and promise that we'd always be friends no matter what. We even drew blood from our fingers and mixed it all together. We were closer than sisters." Lucretia sighed.

"What happened?" Edward asked.

"After I left for Hollywood, I never went back. I was so busy making movies, and my parents had moved away. Then my career failed, and I was embarrassed." Lucretia shrugged. "I was always sorry that I never got in touch with them again. Polly and Sarah. Two of the best friends you could ever have."

"Where are they now?" Edward asked dutifully.

"I have no idea," Lucretia said sadly. "If they were alive and I knew where they were, I'd invite them to our wedding."

Spare me, Edward thought, but he reached over and put his arm around Lucretia. "I'm sure they'd be happy to know that you're happy."

"I know this much: They'd be surprised that I'm marrying you."

Edward didn't quite know how to take that. But he did know that he wanted to do anything he could to delay their arrival at the winery. "Why don't we stop for lunch along the way?" he asked. "Just the two of us. Our last meal alone before we tie the knot."

Lucretia smiled up at him. "Our last meal alone."

33

At their home in the mountains above San Luis Obispo, Lucretia's two childhood friends stared at the television.

"Can you believe her?" Polly asked, shaking her head that had been covered with white hair for over thirty years now. "She's doing it again, and we're not invited."

"Well," Sarah replied as she rocked in her chair. "We didn't invite her to either of our weddings. She got too big for her britches." Sarah leaned in closer to the television set. "Can you believe how young that guy is? It's a shame."

"I wouldn't mind stepping out with a young guy," Polly shot back. "Nothing wrong with that."

"Oh, I suppose not."

The announcer urged viewers to e-mail their thoughts on anything they'd seen on the newscast to the address scrolling across the screen.

Polly and Sarah looked at each other. They'd been living together for fifteen years, since both of their husbands had died. They had many hobbies, liked to take long walks, and lately had become fond of the Internet.

"Why don't we send an e-mail to Lucretia?" Polly suggested.

"What will we say?"

"Remember us?"

They both laughed.

Polly got up from her chair and walked over to an antique hutch. She opened a drawer and shuffled through a pile of pictures. "Here we are." She stared at the image of three teenage girls, their arms around each other and smiling at the camera. She handed it to Sarah.

"Remember the secret the three of us had?"

"How could I forget?"

"A lot of time has passed."

"Sure has."

They both ran to the computer and fired off an e-mail to Lucretia in care of the news channel. They had no doubt they would hear back from her.

34

When Regan stepped outside, the sun's rays warmed her face. If it weren't for this class, I'd go for a walk through the vineyards, she thought. But she wanted to check out Earl's class, so she walked across the parking lot to the little cluster of buildings opposite the main lodge. The architecture reminded her of an old cowboy movie. She could just picture riding a horse up the dirt road, sliding down out of the saddle, and hitching the reins to a post the way cowboys seemed to do so easily in those old westerns. But there wasn't a horse in sight. The only animal nearby was Lilac's cat, sitting in the shade of one of the lemon trees looking bored.

My first meditation class, she thought as she stepped into the wooden structure with a sign above the door that read DEEP BREATHS. Regan had taken plenty of aerobics and stretch classes at the gym, but never yoga or meditation. The screen door slammed behind her, disturbing the early morning quiet. She jumped and looked around.

Now I really need some relaxation, she thought. Off to the right was a spacious room that resembled a dancer's studio, with its polished wood floors and mirrored walls. A black barre ran the length of the far wall, reminding Regan of the ballet class Nora had enrolled her in when she was five. Regan remembered hanging on to the barre as she attempted to shuffle her little slippered feet in the directions commanded by her teacher, who turned out to be a monster. After a couple of lessons Regan bailed out, and Nora signed her up to learn how to play the piano. Another lost cause.

The women Regan had seen earlier were sitting cross-legged on mats chatting quietly. Regan took a mat from the pile in the corner and dragged it over to what she considered was an appropriate distance from a fellow meditator. Four or five other people wandered in after Regan, including the guy who had come into the lodge last night, the only other visitor. What was his name again? Oh, yes, Regan remembered. It was Don.

"Hello," she said.

He nodded back and quickly shut his eyes.

I guess he's really into this, Regan thought. She was surprised. She wasn't quite sure why, but he just didn't seem the type for meditation. Maybe it was because of his tough guy appearance.

Earl appeared in the doorway and made an entrance befitting the Dalai Lama. As he swept across the room, he chanted, "We live in a time when there are many ways available to us to make our bodies comfortable. Good food, good wine . . ."

There's the plug for the wine, Regan thought.

" . . . creature comforts are plentiful. But we still experience stress and suffering. I say that we must slow down and focus our awareness. Our busy lives agitate our minds. We are here to relax our body and calm our mind. I want you all to take off your shoes and socks and lay back on the mats."

It took Regan a few moments to unlace her sneakers. While she did so, she glanced over at Don. The T-shirt he was wearing rode up as he stretched out on the mat, revealing a taut stomach covered with blond hair. Regan found herself staring at the tattoo of a skull and crossbones just below his navel. How special, she thought. She then looked at the mass of thick black hair clinging to his skull. She hadn't really had a close look at him last night across the candlelit room, but she had sensed that his hair was dyed. It's more than that, she thought. He's wearing a wig and a lousy one at that. Why would he go so dark when the rest of the world usually lightens up? He was a natural blond, as they say.

As though sensing her gaze, Don opened his eyes. For an instant the look on his face was downright hostile. But then he attempted a weak smile as he pulled down his shirt. Regan did her best to pretend she hadn't been staring at him. Her heart started pumping a little bit faster as she lay back, just a foot from this curious stranger. Come on, Earl, she thought. Make me feel harmonious. I'm getting edgy here.

Earl inserted a cassette into the stereo. The sounds of waterfalls and rushing water, accompanied by music designed to inspire tranquillity, filled the room.

"Your mind is like a monkey, swinging uncontrollably from branch to branch," Earl began.

I'll say, Regan thought.

"Meditation gently returns your mind to one focus of attention."

Like where the heck Whitney is, Regan wondered.

"Our minds jump back and forth all day long. Memories, worries, thoughts, feelings. Flit, flit, flit. We must slow down the monkey. We must make friends with ourselves. We must smile into our internal organs."

Huh? Regan thought.

"I want you all to close your eyes. We are going to concentrate on letting go of the tension in our bodies so we just melt into the floor. Start by focusing on your breath. Breathe deeply. In . . . out . . . in . . . out. Now I want you to wiggle your toes. Wiggle . . . wiggle . . . wiggle. . . . Become aware of every part of your body."

For the next hour Regan followed Earl's instructions as he led them through a series of stretches and poses and lunges, ending up in the lotus position. She tried her best to get into a relaxed state of mind, but all she could think about was Whitney and her dress being left behind in the driveway. What had happened?

With a few minutes left, Earl turned out the lights. "I want you to clear your mind of all thoughts," he said. "Take a deep, deep breath . . . and another . . . and another. Very good. Now just a reminder: Candles and incense are available next door. Use them to set up a little meditation center in your own home."

Business is business, Regan thought.

The lights were barely back on when Don stood up, slipped into his shoes, and picked up his mat. Regan watched as he deposited it back in the pile in the corner and hurried out of the room. He doesn't seem so relaxed, either, she thought.

And what was he doing with that god-awful hairpiece?

35

Phyllis was utterly depressed. And more than a little nervous. After Lucretia left, Phyllis sat in the kitchen, not knowing what to do.

Phyllis expected $200,000 in "commissions" once Lilac and her family made it to the wedding. Her plan had been so perfect! Better than any game show past or present. Entice the family to the wedding by secretly telling them Lucretia is planning to give them $2 million each, but only if they show up, then convince Lilac to get them all to give Phyllis money "off the top" for her assistance, and everybody's happy. So what if Lucretia was planning to give them the money no matter what? When you're getting $2 million, what's $50,000 more or less?

The way Phyllis saw it, Lucretia wanted nothing more than to have Haskell's family at the wedding. When it became clear to Phyllis that Lilac had no intention of making the effort to attend, Phyllis cooked up her scheme, a scheme that ensured the family would show up in their Sunday best, which would make Lucretia very happy. Phyllis felt she deserved to be paid for that. Lilac had promised to keep their agreement quiet. It wasn't really that hard because if it looked as if Lilac and her family were showing up just for the money, it would make them look bad, too.

But now that they were all going to be together at the winery, Phyllis was afraid that what she had done might leak out. Lilac might say something about the money by mistake. Or, who knows, maybe even intentionally. If she did, Phyllis would lose her commission, and Lucretia would probably fire her.

Phyllis made herself a cup of tea and flipped on the television to the Game Show channel. They were playing reruns of game shows from way back when. Dick Clark's *$25,000 Pyramid* was being broadcast. It was the bonus round, and the winning contestant was being fed clues by a celebrity whose name Phyllis couldn't remember. The contestant had to figure out what all the clues had in common.

"Why you get a loan . . . why you hock your jewelry . . . why you tell your spouse to get a job . . . why you . . ."

"Things you do when you're broke!" Phyllis yelled at the television just as the doorbell rang. "I should know."

Phyllis took a quick sip of her tea. Probably more wedding nonsense, she thought. She walked slowly through the living room and admired how clean it was. See if they can get somebody else to keep this house as nice as I do, she thought.

When Phyllis opened the door, she was surprised to find the reporter who interviewed Lucretia yesterday and a cameraman. The reporter was smiling and blond, and looked as if she was just so happy.

"Hi, there," the woman began.

Phyllis stared at her blankly. She hadn't cleaned up the tomatoes yet, and the woman was standing to one side of them. So was the cameraman.

"I'm Lynne B. Harrison from GOS News. We did the story on Miss Standish yesterday. I was wondering if we could talk to her for a few minutes."

"She's not here," Phyllis stated. "And thanks to your story, somebody threw tomatoes at the front door. Luckily, they only reached the porch." She looked down. Lynne B. Harrison followed her gaze.

"I see that," Lynne said, and with a hand motion she urged the cameraman to record the stewed-looking tomatoes. "You think someone who saw our show did that?"

"Definitely."

"What a shame," Lynne commented, stalling for time, desperately trying to think of a way to get inside. She knew that any new angle would please her boss. She had to get something. "We received hundreds of nice e-mails saying that people were happy Lucretia had found love again. I must say others were a little upset about all the money she made off a dot-com that went bankrupt. I even have an e-mail here for Lucretia from two of her childhood friends. They'd like to talk to her about a secret they have with her that they've kept quiet about for more than seventy years."

Phyllis's eyes almost popped out of her head. She suddenly felt a protectiveness toward Lucretia. Bad enough that everybody, including herself, was trying to get their hands on her money. But if someone was going to embarrass Lucretia in public . . .

"I'll give you an interview if you hand over the e-mail and let Lucretia and no one else contact her friends," Phyllis bargained. Maybe this would be a way to stay in Lucretia's good graces. Heck, Lucretia might even give her a bonus for being so loyal and protective.

Lynne knew she had no choice. She could sit outside in the truck waiting for Lucretia, but she had no idea where Lucretia was. This e-mail could easily be a hoax. There were plenty of kooks who wanted to claim they had a close association with someone in the limelight—what people will do for their fifteen minutes of fame. And her boss wanted something on the air today. A tour of Lucretia's house would be perfect. Lynne handed the printed e-mail to the maid.

"Come on in," Phyllis urged, pulling the door wide open.

36

After the meditation class, Regan wandered next door to the building that housed the combination gift shop and tasting room. The space was airy and rustic. An old-fashioned register sat on one side of a long wooden counter. Several stools were perched in front of the counter. Wineglasses lined the shelves behind, and bottles of wine were displayed in glass cases along the brick wall. Candles and incense and bric-a-brac abounded. Soft classical music was playing in the background. At one end of the room, a round oak table was set with wineglasses of varying sizes and shapes. A sliding glass door at the back of the room opened onto a patio with several picnic tables.

Bella was sitting behind the register. She greeted Regan. "Welcome to our tasting room and gift shop. If I can be of service, please don't hesitate to ask."

"Thank you," Regan answered, thinking that Bella suddenly seemed a little strange. Her singsongy voice and her glassy-eyed stare gave Regan the impression that she was a few cards short of a full deck.

A brochure in front of the register caught Regan's eye. She walked over and picked up a copy of *Altered States—A Look Back*. Black-and-white pictures taken at the turn of the century filled the pages. Many of the pictures looked the same. Trees and more trees.

"I understand your grandfather once owned this winery," Regan remarked to Bella.

"Prohibition ruined it for him," Bella said with disgust. "You know there are a lot of us whose families really had it bad when Prohibition was passed." She stared up at Regan, a sudden fire in her eyes. "Quite frankly, I think the government should compensate us for our ancestors' troubles."

Oh, brother, Regan thought as the theme music to the *Twilight Zone* started playing in her head.

"I mean, for God's sake, if the government hadn't passed that stupid law, this would all be mine right now."

Regan wondered if Bella had discussed this with Lilac before she was hired. Regan guessed not.

"Well," Regan countered, thinking of Lucretia, "look at what happened with the dot-coms. Fifty years from now there will be people saying they would be rich if only their grandparents had gotten out before they crashed."

Bella shook her head dismissively. "Not the same thing."

"I understand some people say the property is haunted by a ghost. Do you know any stories from the days your grandfather owned the winery?"

"All I know is that he had to run away because of his debts. It wasn't right what happened. It just wasn't right."

So why would you come back here, Regan wondered. It's not going to evoke happy memories. Regan smiled inwardly. Bella could use a class or two with Earl.

A couple wandered in, and Bella welcomed them as she had Regan a few minutes before. The same words, the same inflections. It was like the recording at the airport that told you to load and unload fast, or your car would be towed.

Regan still had the brochure in her hand. "How much is this?"

"It's free of charge," Bella said, her bowed lips forming a smile.

"Thanks. I'll see you later." Regan wandered back outside just as her parents were pulling up the dirt road.

"You made good time," Regan noted as Luke stopped the car a few feet in front of her. "Why don't we just go into town for lunch right now?" Regan felt unsettled and wanted to talk to her parents in peace before they checked into the B and B and she had to introduce them to Lilac.

"Sure, honey," Nora agreed quickly, sensing Regan's concern. "We had a light breakfast. I'm kind of hungry."

Regan opened the door and got in the backseat. She considered going in to tell Lilac she was leaving for lunch but figured Lilac would never notice. If she's not worried about her daughter, she certainly won't worry about me.

37

Ricky woke up feeling almost human. He thought he actually might be able to down a piece of toast. Although he was still weak, he forced himself to get out of bed and turn on the shower.

The water felt good on his achy, dehydrated body. He opened his mouth, welcoming the stream of liquid that wet his face and relieved his parched lips. He grabbed the shampoo bottle and lathered up. It was as if he were cleansing away all the previous day's ailments. Three minutes later he reluctantly turned off the faucets and grabbed a towel. Already I feel 100 percent better, he thought. Not well enough to go for a run as he usually did on a Saturday morning, but much better nonetheless.

Ricky was twenty-two years old, and exercising every day was part of his routine. His body was compact, 5 feet 7 inches tall, with a slight but muscular build. He had curly dark hair and olive skin, and was considered pretty cute by a lot of the girls he met.

He dressed in jeans and a T-shirt and headed out the door. It was a beautiful day, and he definitely had cabin fever. He had to get out, even if just for a little while.

The hotel lobby was quiet. No one was around. Ricky walked down to the coffee shop on the corner and had a light breakfast, toast and tea—what his mother had always given him when he was sick. It was as satisfying as any meal he'd ever eaten. After Ricky paid his check, he stood outside and weighed his options. I don't feel well enough to run or ride my bike, but I want to do something. I know: I'll go up to Norman's and collect my money. Maybe he'll even let me sit in on the seminar. If I'm recommending his seminars to people, I should know what they're all about.

Quickly he turned on his heel and headed for the hotel parking lot, thinking that it would be fun to see Whitney off the set and to see who else was in the class. Maybe there'd be some good-looking girls. Ricky and his girlfriend had broken up recently because he was away from Los Angeles so much.

"I'm too young to put up with these long separations," she'd explained as she fluffed up her hair and reapplied her makeup. "I'm in my prime. I need someone who is there for me, Ricky—there for me when I need it most. Sometimes I just need a hug. Ya know?"

"Yeah," Ricky had said as he walked out the door.

Now as he got in his car, he felt energized. This will be fun, he thought. I'll meet some new people. He was also honest enough to admit to himself that what he was most looking forward to was seeing Whitney. If only she weren't involved with Frank Kipsman. He laughed. Maybe one day she'll fall for my charm.

He inserted a CD into the stereo system and headed for the hills. Norman's house was on a beautiful spot up in the heavily wooded mountains. It was such a great day for a drive. If he had turned on the news in the car instead of listening to music, he might have changed his mind.

Wildfires were on the way.

38

In the little village near Altered States, the dining choices were limited. Since Luke and Nora had done enough driving for one day, they didn't feel like venturing into another town. There was one pub, Muldoon's, that Regan guessed was probably where Bella's husband was employed. A sign in the window advertised grilled cheese and tomato sandwiches.

"Do you want to try this place?" Regan asked. "It looks like it has a little local flavor."

"Grilled cheese and tomato was always a favorite of mine," Luke said dryly as he parked the car in front.

Inside, the jukebox was playing a Roy Orbison song. It wasn't yet noon, so they had their choice of tables. They took a booth by the window that had a view of the mountains in the distance. Muldoons was a typical pub with a darkened interior and the smell of aged beer in the air.

A waitress came over to take their order. They had all decided to try the specialty of the house.

"Good choice," the waitress commented. Her name tag read SANDY. She was probably about sixty and had a leathery face that looked as if it had been tanned since she was twelve. "What about a drink? We have a special beer . . ."

"What kind of wine do you have by the glass?" Nora asked.

The waitress practically snorted. "You mean by the jug? You might be in wine country, but the owner of this joint could care less. He buys wine in vats the size of a watercooler. Take my word for it, it's not from a winery that won any medals."

Regan grabbed the opportunity to try to get some information. "We're staying up at Altered States," she volunteered.

Sandy made a face. "That place."

Regan smiled. "What do you mean?"

"There's been a lot of hard luck up there. The owner who had it when Prohibition started was run out of town. Then it was just abandoned for years. Everyone says it has a ghost. The last owners went bankrupt. Now that family who owns it are into all that meditation and incense. Why don't they just concentrate on making good wine?"

Regan thought of Leon's impatience with Earl. "One of the family members has been into meditation for a long time."

"Earl."

"Yes, Earl."

"He lived off the fat of the land at another meditation center until they finally booted him out. He worked around the grounds and doing odd jobs, but there wasn't enough for him to do to warrant free room and board for the rest of his enlightened life."

"I thought he was in the oil business."

"Could have fooled me. If he was, it must have been a long time ago."

Nora and Luke were just taking all of this in. They knew when Regan was on one of her fishing expeditions, and they loved to listen.

"You seem to know a lot about them," Regan noted.

"I've lived around here my whole life. You get to know what's going on. When I was a kid, we went up to Altered States at night when it was abandoned and scared ourselves silly. We'd go into the old barn at the far end of the property and tell each other ghost stories. And I've been working in this pub for years. Working in a pub, you hear about everybody's business."

"A woman who works at Altered States in the gift shop said that it was her grandfather who had owned it when Prohibition was passed."

"Her husband just got a job here." Sandy lowered her voice. "He applies for a job as a bartender, and they hire him without asking too many questions. The other day I asked him to make me a Singapore Sling. He looked at me like I had two heads. Do I look like I have two heads?"

"No," Regan answered dutifully.

"That's right, I don't. What bartender worth his salt doesn't know how to make a drink like that? Now, speaking of drinks, what are you all drinking?"

The three of them ordered iced tea.

When Sandy walked away, Nora said to Regan, "We had a lovely dinner with Wally and Bev last night. He said he knows the director of the movie Whitney is in."

Regan shook her head. She explained to her parents everything that had happened that morning. "I won't feel relieved until I know that Whitney pulled out of the driveway this morning by herself."

Sandy brought them their iced tea.

Regan's mind was "swinging from branch to branch." From Whitney to Bella to Bella's husband, who sounded as though he, too, was a few cards short of a full deck. Then an image flashed in her mind: the skull and crossbones tattoo. There's something about that guy, Regan thought. There's something about him that's just not right.

39

Lucretia and Edward ate lunch at a roadside diner filled with tattooed motorcyclists whose gleaming bikes were lined up outside the restaurant door. Lucretia was sorry they didn't have a camera to take a picture of her in the Rolls-Royce parked next to all the Harley-Davidsons.

As they munched on cheeseburgers at the counter, Lucretia said coyly, "Darling, I know you want it to be a surprise, but I'm dying to find out where you're taking me on our honeymoon."

"You'll have to wait until tomorrow afternoon when we leave the wedding reception. You know it's a road trip, and that's all I'm telling you," Edward said, trying to sound in charge. "Just be sure to bring all kinds of clothes." Edward knew that he couldn't tell Lucretia he was taking her to Denver where the altitude would make it difficult for her to breathe. He wanted to wear her out, but he didn't want to make it obvious to other people. He'd be sure they stopped in other cities as well. At night when she was asleep he planned to sneak out and have a good time. He wanted to stay away as long as possible and not come back until the excitement of the wedding died down.

On the television, perched high in the corner above a glass case of cakes and pies, Phyllis's face suddenly filled the screen.

She was standing in Lucretia's living room next to the reporter who had done the story on the impending nuptials.

"We are now in the home of former silent screen star Lucretia Standish," Lynne B. Harrison reported as she held up a gilt-framed picture of Lucretia that normally rested on the coffee table. "Lucretia made over fifty million dollars off a dot-com she had invested in and then most wisely cashed out of."

"Turn up the volume," Lucretia screeched to the waitress.

Noting Lucretia's desperation—or perhaps because she never wanted to hear a sound like Lucretia screaming again—the waitress quickly complied.

"Lucky Lucretia is getting married tomorrow, and we are here live with her housekeeper, Phyllis. Phyllis, what can you tell us about Lucretia and her fiancé? Do they seem happy to you?"

Phyllis turned to face the camera directly. Edward felt as if she were looking at him alone. His whole body tensed.

"Oh, yes," Phyllis answered amiably. "They're nutty about each other."

Edward relaxed.

"What can you tell us about him?"

Edward tensed up again.

"Not much," she acknowledged. "I don't really know him. But I'm certainly looking forward to getting to know him."

"Wonderful. Now can we take a look in the backyard where the wedding will take place?"

"Of course."

The camera followed Phyllis and Lynne out to the pool area where dozens of round tables were being set up by the caterer. A trellis was being decorated with ribbons and flowers. Workers were putting down a dance floor at the end of the yard. A fountain was being hauled in, presumably for the champagne.

Lucretia clapped her hands. "Look, darling, look. They're getting it all ready for tomorrow."

"I can't wait," Edward said fervently.

"This is going to be a beautiful wedding," Lynne said enthusiastically. "I wish we could talk to Lucretia again, but I know she's off at a secret location resting up for her big day. Viewers, please let us know your thoughts on Lucretia Standish's wedding to Edward Fields. Do you think a forty-seven-year age difference is too much? Or does love win out? We'll be back later with more on the plans for the big day."

Lucretia turned to Edward and smiled. "Darling, we're the 'It' couple of the weekend, aren't we? You don't think a forty-seven-year age difference is too much, do you?" she asked coquettishly.

You must be crazy! he wanted to shout. Instead, he smiled and said, "I think it's just about right. A fifty-year age difference might be overdoing it, but forty-seven works perfectly for us."

"I agree," Lucretia said, looking slightly troubled for the briefest moment. Then she blurted, "Let's call Phyllis from the car phone. I want to find out what else is going on down there."

"Maybe we should go back home," Edward suggested eagerly, deciding that might be the lesser of two evils.

"No! I promised we'd spend the night with my family at the winery. Besides, there's such a thing as overexposure. The news station is covering the wedding tomorrow. That's enough. Now pay the check, darling, and let's go."

Lucretia jumped down off the stool and turned to look at the roomful of bikers. They had all been watching the television and now turned their attention to her.

"Way to go, Lucretia," one of them yelled. "Want a ride on my bike?"

"I'd love one," she cried, clearly thrilled at the attention.

The group broke into applause, and several bikers whistled loudly, deafening sounds that must have impaired the hearing of everyone in the joint.

"Lucretia," Edward protested.

"Edward, just once around the block," she said firmly.

Two of the bikers escorted the couple outside.

"My name is Dirt," said the burly guy who had offered Lucretia a ride. He wore a sleeveless leather vest, his enormous muscular arms were covered with tattoos, and he was wearing a bandana around his balding head. "Allow me." Effortlessly he lifted up an adoring Lucretia and placed her on the back of his bike. He hopped on, kicked it to start, and off they went amid the sound of a revving motor.

"And my name is Big Shot," the overdeveloped creature next to Edward announced. "And we just want you to know that if we hear about any funny business having to do with your wedding to that little lady, we're going to come get you and make you pay." He paused and smiled, revealing the most dentally challenged arrangement of teeth Edward had ever seen. "We don't like it when people take advantage of little old ladies. Understand?"

Edward hoped Big Shot couldn't see or hear his knees knocking together. "I'll take special care of her," he said earnestly. "Really special care."

Big Shot started to laugh, a sound not unlike a low menacing growl. "That's good. Cause we'll be watching."

And it was my idea to stop for lunch, Edward realized miserably as he noticed Big Shot's huge arms and legs. He, too, was clad in a sleeveless vest and denim shorts. It was hard to tell where one of his tattoos began and another ended.

A moment later Lucretia and Dirt vroomed back into the parking lot. "Darling," Lucretia cried. "These nice boys are coming to the wedding!"

40

Whitney was miserable. She was thirsty, and her whole body was sore from being tied up for hours now. Have I been left here to die? she wondered. When will someone find me?

As she lay in the back of her Jeep, she tried to think of all the reasons someone would want her out of the way. If her captor wanted to kill her, he could have done it immediately. It was more likely that she was being kidnapped, but why? Was he going to ask for a ransom? Did he know that the family would soon be millionaires?

Almost no one outside the immediate family knew about the money. Who could her captor be? Could it be the guy who was in the dining room last night? Whitney wondered. He could have overheard when we were talking. But if he overheard their conversation, he would have known that they weren't getting the money unless they went to the wedding. Whitney remembered that he went out for a walk after dinner and was gone for a while. Maybe he roamed around the property and found this old barn.

Suddenly she could hear the sound of the door opening. Her heart started pounding. Was he going to kill her? She held her breath. Then, just as quickly as the door opened, it was shut.

Oh my God! Whitney thought. Was it him? Was it someone else? Frantically, she twisted from side to side, trying to thump the side of the car's interior with her legs. She grunted, and the gag in her mouth felt as if it would choke her. It must have been someone else, she thought with a mixture of frustration and hope. But who? No one ever came out here. The old barn was at the far edge of the property.

Her cell phone started ringing in her purse on the front seat. Whitney sighed. Whoever you are calling, why couldn't you have called a minute ago? Maybe the person who was here a minute ago would have heard the phone ring.

I've got to stop struggling and preserve my energy, Whitney realized, so I can be ready if someone who can help me comes back. I'll have to use every ounce of strength I can muster to make my presence in this creaky old barn known.

41

Shovel in hand, Bella went around the back of the big barn and once again started to break ground. For the past week she'd been spending her lunch hours digging up the area behind the barn, hunting for her grandfather Ward's buried treasure. She didn't know exactly what it would turn out to be, but one thing she did know was that it belonged to her family, no matter who owned the property.

Grandpa Ward had settled in Canada after he hightailed it out of California. Not long after he landed in British Columbia, he met and married Bella's grandmother. Never again did he set foot on U.S. soil. Bella's mother, Rose, was born several years later, and when she was a young girl, she'd sit on Ward's knee, listening to the same stories over and over. "I loved my winery," he'd say. "If only Prohibition hadn't been passed . . ."

"If it weren't for Prohibition, we'd never have met," his wife reminded him more than once.

"We would so have met," he replied, waving away her argument, sometimes with a laugh. "You, my dear, were born under a lucky star. We were meant to be. My winery, that's what wasn't meant to be. If only Prohibition hadn't been passed . . ."

If only, if only, if only. The family lived in Vancouver, and

Ward had gotten a job on one of the fishing boats. "Someday I'll go back," he said. But he'd died young, before Prohibition even ended.

Bella's grandmother had never gone through all of Ward's old papers. And Bella's mother, Rose, cut from the same cloth, didn't look at them, either. When her mother died, Rose just stored the family archives in her attic. "Your grandfather was such a pack rat. There are too many boxes," she'd tell Bella. "Because he had to leave California with nothing, from then on he decided to keep everything—and I mean everything. Someday I'll sort through his things."

"Someday" ended up being a month ago when Rose decided to join several of her friends in an extended living complex. Her husband was gone, and she was anxious for company. So Bella, who should have gotten a job as a closet organizer, had gone to Vancouver to help her mother clean out the house. Bella was brutal when it came to tossing things out. "Get rid of it," Bella ordered her mother without a second thought every time Rose held up an object being considered for the trash bin.

Rose could bring only a few pieces of furniture to her new home. After much debate it was finally settled that the cuckoo clock and her La-Z-Boy recliner would make the cut. Bella was never so happy as when she carried Rose's green shag rug out to the sidewalk, to be hauled off by the trashman. Other tired furniture followed.

Finally they attacked the attic. Bella, being Bella, rolled up her sleeves and ripped open the cardboard boxes with gusto. Old magazines and newspapers filled many of the cartons.

Rose shook her head. "Dad hated to throw away a magazine or a newspaper before he read it cover to cover."

Bella tossed one periodical after another into a garbage bag, sneezing several times from the decades-old dust.

One box contained old photos, which meant a slight delay in productivity.

"Will you look at him?" Rose marveled. "He was such a natty dresser."

The photo showed Ward dressed in a white linen suit, standing at a beachfront cafe, sipping a glass of wine, and tipping his straw hat to whoever was taking the picture.

Bella glanced at the picture and smiled, but within two seconds she was ripping open another carton. This one was filled with letters and old yellowed documents. Bella pulled out a notebook and opened it to the first page. There were several scrawled notations and a headline, IMPRESSIONS. Quickly she turned the pages and found sentences and phrases scribbled willy-nilly.

"Mom, listen to this!" Bella cried excitedly.

Rose stopped and cocked her head as Bella read aloud Ward's diary. It was mostly about his winery—how he loved the smell of the vineyards, the feel of the grapes in his hands, the taste of the wine in his mouth. One page read simply, "Smell, swirl, sip, swish, swallow. What could be better?"

Toward the back of the notebook the tone of the pages changed: Have to get out of town. No use. Can't keep the place up. Tried to get the church to buy my wine for sacramental purposes but no luck. It's the only wine that's legal now. I'll have to run. Just buried my treasures and hope one day to come back for them.

Bella dropped the notebook when she read that last line.

"What treasures?" Rose cried as Bella leaned down to pick up the notebook. A piece of paper had fallen out, and Bella scooped it up.

"I don't know," Bella said as she unfolded the stray paper. Then she gasped, "A map of fortune! This is a map of Grandpa's winery, and it's dated 1920. It gives the exact address, and there's an X marked where he says buried treasure! And listen to this . . ."

"I'm still listening, dear."

"Grandpa wrote something on the bottom of the page:

Because I was forced to get out of town fast—thanks to my awful debts—I couldn't take everything that was near and dear to me. So I buried my precious cache at the edge of the property, behind the old barn. I hope to go back one day and reclaim my treasures. But if someone is reading this after I die, and I never did get back, then you may as well go hunt for it yourself! The buried treasure is all yours.

"This is amazing!" Bella exclaimed. "Didn't he tell you or Grandma about the treasure?"

"He died unexpectedly. He was still a young man. He always said he wanted to go back to California one day when he had enough money."

Mother and daughter were uncharacteristically silent for a moment.

"I wish I were well enough to do some digging," Rose said half-jokingly.

"I'm going," Bella declared. "I have to go!"

"But the treasure might be gone, and somebody else must own the winery now."

"So what! I'll figure something out. Whatever is still there belongs to you and me."

"And I suppose Walter," Rose said, shaking her head.

Bella had married Walter, an American, whom Rose had never particularly approved of. They lived in the state of Washington. Walter had just lost his job with an airline company. Bella had a lot of motivation to go to central California and hunt for the treasure that she hoped would be a bonanza.

"He'll come with me," Bella said.

"What if he doesn't want to?"

"He has no choice."

That was only four weeks ago. Now, after having managed to become employed at the winery, Bella was spending another lunch hour digging for who knows what. No one had seen her at the back edge of the property, and no one questioned the fact that she liked to take a walk during her free time. If they caught her digging, Bella had concocted a story about rearranging the dirt because according to legend it would bring good luck to the winery. She figured they were hippieish enough to go for that mumbo jumbo.

Walter told her he couldn't help her dig because of his bad back. "It's tied up in knots like a pretzel," he complained. So Bella made him get a job as a bartender that he'd keep until she found the treasure and they could return home. She said it made them look more respectable than if he sat in their rented room watching television all day. Begrudgingly, Walter agreed to the plan. But now he was actually enjoying his job at the pub.

"Just don't get arrested," he cautioned his wife.

The land behind the barn sloped down to a creek that ran the length of the property. After nearly an hour of digging, Bella was still coming up with nothing but dirt, worms, and rocks. She dropped the shovel and wandered down to the creek where she cooled her hands in the clear, sparkling water.

"That feels good," she said aloud. Her hands were developing calluses, and they were tired and achy and smelled like sweet perfume. Bella couldn't stand the fragrance of all the scented candles and incense in the gift shop, but she had to grin and bear it. She needed a reason for being on the property every day.

After a few moments Bella stood and started to walk back toward the main house. She started to turn back, realizing she had forgotten to put the shovel back in the barn. Oh, well, she thought. It doesn't really matter. I'll be back here tomorrow.

She smiled. That shovel is so old anyway. I wonder if it belonged to Grandpa Ward—in which case it's now mine.

42

Rex had run to his car as soon as the meditation class ended. Even though he had made the decision to stick around the winery and was now waiting for Eddie to get there with the "love of his life," he still felt like a caged rat. He was nervous about his cohorts in New York. And all the stories about Eddie and Lucretia on the television were really making Rex anxious. If they start snooping into Eddie's past too much, Rex knew his name might pop up—and not in the most flattering way.

Rex drove down to the little village, his sense of unease growing by the minute. He walked around, wandering in and out of the stores. That took about ten minutes. He thought about going into the pub and getting a drink, but he nixed that idea when he saw Regan Reilly get out of a car with some people and head inside Muldoon's. The sight of her made him more agitated. He thought about Whitney tied up in her Jeep. Don't worry, he told himself. I won't get caught. After Eddie is married, we'll call from a pay phone and let Whitney's family know where she is. Maybe they won't even have missed her for that long.

Rex went into the deli on Main Street and ordered a turkey sandwich on whole wheat bread. "Make that two," he said suddenly, deciding that he would go back to the barn and give Whitney something to eat and drink. He'd also give her a chance to go to the bathroom. The barn was big, and there was an ancient toilet in a little closet at one end of the large room. She'd just better not try anything.

I'm not such a bad guy, he thought. I'm just trying to make my way in the cold, cruel world. He grinned as he took a couple of sodas and bottled water from the refrigerator case. It's just when people get in my way . . .

"Would you like potato chips or pickles with your sandwiches?" the deli man asked sincerely.

"Potato chips."

"Very good, sir. Potato chips it is."

"Could I have two separate bags please?"

"My pleasure. I hope you're going to go out and enjoy this beautiful day."

"I plan to," Rex answered in a manner that discouraged further pleasantries.

The items were bagged, Rex paid, and out the door he went. This is a pretty little place, he thought, admiring the mountains that seemed to stand guard around the town. Very different from Manhattan. He got in his car and drove to a tiny park down the block. He ate in the car, with all the windows rolled down and the radio on. The sandwich tasted good, and the soft drink was cold and refreshing. When he finished the potato chips, he crumbled the bag and stuffed it into one of the grocery sacks.

On his way back to Altered States, he decided that the safest thing would be to drive back to the main lodge and then walk to the barn. If he brought his car out to the barn and someone noticed, it would seem suspicious. It would also draw unwanted attention to the site. Definitely not what he wanted.

All was quiet in the parking lot. Rex took the bag with

Whitney's sandwich and bottle of water, and quickly crossed the lot to the fields. As far as the eye could see there were rows and rows of tall oak trees. He quickened his pace and hurried as fast as he could without running, just in case someone came by. The barn sat at the base of the mountain and couldn't be seen from the main lodge.

When Rex finally reached the barn, he heard a scraping sound around the back. His heart stopped. He waited. Not hearing anything more, he silently crept along the side of the barn. All he could hear was the running creek. Cautiously he stole a glance behind the barn. Piles of dirt had been dug up, and there was a woman kneeling by the water!

Rex tried to maintain his cool as he hurried back toward the front of the barn and kept going. Who is she? he wondered frantically as he moved to the protection of a group of trees nearby. And just what is she doing back there?

43

On the way back to the winery, Regan's cell phone rang. It was Jack. Regan was amused that Nora and Luke stopped talking the minute they realized who was calling.

"What's going on?" Jack asked.

"A few developments. My parents are with me—they're going to spend the night at Altered States. Lucretia and her fiancé are coming up as well, which should be interesting." Regan didn't add, "Wish you were here," because her parents were hanging on every word.

"They're coming up the day before the wedding?"

"Apparently Lucretia's gotten a lot of unwanted attention from the television piece. She needs to relax."

"Maybe you'll get an invitation to the wedding," Jack said. "Any word about Whitney?"

"No. We just had lunch in town, and I'm about to see her mother. Maybe she called. I hope so."

"I hope so, too." Jack cleared his throat, always a sign to Regan that he had something important to say. "So you'll get to meet Lucretia's fiancé. From what I've found out so far, this Edward Fields is quite a hustler."

"Really?"

"Yes. His first name is Hugo, but he dropped that before he met Lucretia. Now he uses his middle name, Edward. Hugo has quite a history. Over the years he's lived with several older women who have provided for him. He actually had a job on Wall Street ten years ago, but it didn't last. He's enjoyed stints as a fund-raiser for charities where he ended up paying himself great bonuses. He's raised seed money for different companies, such as the one Lucretia got involved in, and collected handsome commissions. He also did some front-running—buying a stock, promoting it so the value goes up, then selling it before anyone else does. Basically he calls himself a consultant. He's a smooth operator, so there's nothing we can pin on him. He's never been convicted of a crime. Lucretia is his big catch. After the wedding he'll be able to retire. His favorite hobby is gambling. Let's just hope he doesn't lose all of her money at the craps tables or the track."

Regan sighed. "There are so many of those con men around. It's unbelievable what they can pull off. And now Hugo's going to get away with taking Lucretia for a ride. Of course there's no law that says you can't marry someone for their money."

"And who wants to be the one to tell the blushing bride that her intended is a gold digger?"

"Shoot the messenger," Regan joked.

"I'll tell you one thing," Jack said. "I bet Hugo's very anxious to get Lucretia down the aisle before there's a messenger who needs to be shot. California is a community property state. Since they've been engaged only two days, I doubt there's much of a prenuptial, if there is one at all."

"Lucretia's only relatives are the winery owners, and she's meeting them for the first time today," Regan mused.

"Eddie must be wishing they never meet at all. Oh, that's another thing. His friends call him Eddie. When he puts up a front, it's Edward."

Something in the back of her mind started to nag at Regan. Whitney wasn't officially missing, but if it turned out that she met with foul play, would Edward have anything to do with it? Did he know that Lucretia was planning to give away millions if all four relatives attended the wedding? "I can't wait until later when we all gather for a glass of wine," Regan said, planning her attack. " 'Tell me about yourself, Edward,' I'll say ever so sweetly."

Jack laughed. "I have faith in your ability to rattle him."

"By the way, how's your case going?"

"We're still questioning the guy we brought in for selling the stolen artwork. He's obviously not working alone. We have a search warrant for his apartment. Detectives are over there right now. Hopefully they'll find something to help us figure out who this guy's cohorts are. Something tells me they're a dangerous crowd. Hold on a second, Regan."

Regan waited, the nagging feeling about Whitney still bothering her.

Jack got back on the line. "I've got to run. I'll call you later."

When Regan hung up, Nora said, "I can't wait to meet this Lucretia."

"And I can't wait to meet her fiancé," Luke added as he turned down the dirt road to Altered States.

"You can ask him his intentions, Dad," Regan said, patting her father on the shoulder.

When they pulled into the parking lot, Lilac came out of the candle shop to greet them. "Welcome," she said with a big smile. "We're so happy to have you at Altered States."

Regan introduced her parents just as Bella was seen emerging from the fields.

"Oh, good," Lilac noted. "Bella's back from her lunch hour. She can take over in the shop, and I'll get you checked in."

"Have you heard from Whitney?" Regan asked.

"No."

"Did the head of the acting seminar call back?"

"Not yet." Lilac seemed unconcerned. "Earl says those kinds of workshops go for hours without stopping for a break."

As they retrieved Luke and Nora's bags from the car, Bella waved to the group and headed straight for the shop. To Regan she looked a little red-faced and winded. There's something about her that I can't put my finger on, Regan thought. Regan shrugged her shoulders. Whitney was her main concern at the moment. I'll put another call through to that acting seminar, she decided. They must have broken for lunch by now.

44

Lucretia's Rolls-Royce was surrounded by twenty-one motorcycles as it traveled up the highway, an escort worthy of any
head of state. Edward tried to pretend he was enjoying the attention, but every time he looked in the rearview mirror, Big
Shot's evil grin unnerved him a little more. Edward was sure
that he had taken the spot directly behind the car for exactly
that reason. Dirt was riding in front of the Rolls, and the rest of
the Road's Scholars, as they called themselves, were in formation all around the car. Not a single one of them would you want
to meet in a dark alley.

"Darling, you said I was fun, didn't you?" Lucretia asked, her
eyes glittering.

"I did say that," Edward agreed, wondering if he would make
it through the weekend alive. I have to call Rex and make sure
he doesn't do anything to harm Whitney, he thought in a panic.
Edward was getting worried. He'd done a lot of dirty deeds in
his life, but putting someone directly in harm's way was never
one of them. The only thing he'd taken aim at, so to speak, were
people's wallets. A trickle of sweat ran down his back, and Edward realized with no uncertainty that he didn't want to get involved in any hard crimes that put people's lives at risk. Not

now. Not with someone like Big Shot riding his tail. He hoped he'd made that clear to Rex.

"Oh, with all this excitement, I haven't called Phyllis yet," Lucretia exclaimed, diving for the phone that was situated between them. She pressed in her Beverly Hills number and put the call on the speakerphone.

Edward felt doomed as they waited for Phyllis to pick up.

"Hello. Standish residence," Phyllis answered in a reluctant tone of voice.

"Phyllis," Lucretia screeched. "Oh my God! I saw you on television. How exciting!"

"You didn't mind?"

"No. The backyard looked beautiful. You should have led the reporter to the wall of pictures of me in my Hollywood days."

"Sorry."

"That's all right. Why did they come back?"

"They're still here," Phyllis whispered. "She just went out to the television van to get something. They've gotten so many calls about the story that they want to do more on you. I tried to say no, but the reporter said that they had gotten an e-mail from two of your childhood friends who say they have a secret they share with you."

"Polly and Sarah!" Lucretia's voice—if possible—went up several octaves.

"So you remember them?"

"Of course I remember them!"

"Do you know what the secret is?"

"Yes." Lucretia's voice broke, and all the gaiety she had been feeling seemed to evaporate.

"Is it bad?" Phyllis asked.

"It could be worse, I suppose."

"Oh, dear. Well, listen, I made the reporter give me the e-mail in return for the interview in the house."

"She's not going to use it?"

"I can't be sure, but I don't think so. Polly and Sarah addressed part of the message directly to you."

"What does it say?" Lucretia's heart was beating wildly.

"Hold on." Phyllis dropped the phone on the counter, lowered the TV, and retrieved the e-mail that she had stuffed in her purse for safekeeping. She also pulled out her eyeglasses and put them on. "Okay. Here goes:

Dear Lukey,

Lucretia screamed.

Phyllis paused.

"Sorry," Lucretia said, recovering quickly. "It's been so long since someone called me that. Please continue."

"Okay," Phyllis said. "One more time:

Dear Lukey,

Remember us? Polly and Sarah? We couldn't believe it when we saw you on television today. It's been so long since you've appeared on any screens anywhere.

"How catty!" Lucretia interrupted.

"Whatever." Phyllis continued:

But you look great, and we wanted to congratulate you on finding a younger man. We know you've done it before! Remember when we came down to Hollywood for your birthday party the day the stock market crashed? What a night that was. Remember the pact we made that very night? We're sure you do. We're sorry we never got to see you much after that. You grew apart from us. Unlike you, we both married only once. Our husbands are gone now. We decided it would be more fun to live together than rock in our chairs alone.

The times we remember most fondly are of the three of us as teenagers going up to the graveyard behind your father's winery. We thought we had our lives figured out, didn't we? We had some great discussions up there.

After we saw you on TV, we started wondering what people would think if they knew about the secret pact we made that night at your birthday party. It makes us giggle.

Lucretia screamed again.

"There's one more line."

"What?"

We'd love it if you got in touch.

"What's their number?" Lucretia asked quickly.

"I don't know."

"Why not?"

"They only gave an e-mail address."

"Where do they live?"

"Doesn't say. Oh—I think the reporter is coming back in."

"Tell her she can have anything!"

"What?"

"I don't want her contacting those two. Put her on the phone."

"All righty." Phyllis handed the phone to Lynne, who was now standing by her side.

"Hello, Lucretia," Lynne began in a falsely cheery tone that grated on Lucretia. "So many people are interested in everything about you. They just can't get enough of this story."

◆

"How flattering," Lucretia replied, willing herself to sound calm and chatty. "We're on our way up to my niece and nephews' winery north of Santa Barbara to have a family get-together before the wedding." She then whispered, "You'll never guess what's going on." She knew she had to give this reporter something to keep her away from Polly and Sarah.

"What?"

"We have a twenty-one-man motorcycle brigade escorting us to the winery. They're all coming to the wedding tomorrow."

"What a great visual," Lynne said excitedly. "Where did you meet them?"

"At a roadside diner."

"I love it! What I'd really love to do is arrange for a camera crew from our affiliate in Santa Barbara to get footage of your arrival at the winery. I just hope they can get there in time."

"You've got at least forty-five minutes," Lucretia said. "I'll tell Edward here to slow down."

Lynne laughed. "Wonderful! Would you mind if I took a ride up there myself? I'd love to interview your relatives."

"Why not?" Lucretia retorted. "The more the merrier."

"Terrific."

"Phyllis will give you the address. Can I speak to her again?"

"Of course."

"Hello, Lucretia."

"Give me that e-mail address. I'll get in touch with those two. I'll use Edward's Blackberry or blueberry or whatever they call those miniature computers."

Edward gasped, then pretended he had a cough.

Phyllis whispered while the reporter was excitedly talking to her boss on her cell phone. "Do you mind if I ask what the secret pact is?"

"I certainly do! Now give me that e-mail address."

When Lucretia hung up on Phyllis, Edward reached for her

hand. "All this talk of a secret. You're going to tell me what it is, aren't you?"

"No! It's a girly thing. It's silly, but I don't want the world to know." Lucretia batted her eyes at him. "Besides, we are all allowed to have a few secrets, aren't we?"

Oh, yes, Edward thought. More than a few. More than you can ever imagine.

45

After Norman spent four hours teaching his students how to tap into their creative powers and discover their own charisma, he felt satisfied. They were a pretty good group. As usual there were one or two students who tried to grab all the attention. It happened at every workshop. Norman once read that when you put together a random bunch of people, certain personality types always emerge. Someone who is a leader in one group might assume a backseat with a different collection of individuals, but somehow all the roles become filled. It was almost as if it were a law of nature. You always have the quiet ones, and a class clown will usually emerge.

"Okay, everyone," he announced. "Lunch is served inside the house. We'll resume in an hour."

Most students opted for the group lunch since they were in a remote spot in the mountains—not to mention that the price of the seminar included meals and a place to stay for the night. Norman had transformed his basement into two dormlike rooms. The seminar didn't end until midnight or one in the morning, and Norman felt that when the students stayed overnight, it helped solidify the work they'd done all day in breaking down their individual barriers and defenses. It was like camp for grown-ups. Norman also felt that it would make the students more appreciative of the comforts of their own beds and their own space, something that could help them as actors.

"Be aware of everything around you," Norman told his students over and over. "When you look at someone, really see them. When you taste a food, really taste it. Remember how it feels to be hot or cold or exhausted. Be specific."

Norman walked out of the backyard and across the barn to his house.

"Norman?"

He turned. It was Adele, one of the attention grabbers. A fiery redhead, she had a great figure and was dressed in one of the most revealing mesh tops he had ever seen. She had also shoehorned herself into a pair of designer blue jeans.

"Yes," he answered warily.

"I feel I'm having such trouble letting go," she pouted. "I mean, I feel my creativity just begging for release, but it's blocked all in here." She put her hands over her chest.

Oh, boy, Norman thought. I don't think you've ever let anything block you. "We'll work on that after lunch," he assured her.

She grabbed his forearm and squeezed her eyes shut. "Thank you. I think this morning has already changed my life."

"That's good," Norman said quickly. "How about lunch?"

Adele opened her eyes. "I have special dietary needs, so I brought my own."

"Terrific," Norman said, managing to break away. It's always the least talented people who make the biggest fuss, he thought. Somehow he knew that Whitney Weldon wasn't like that, and he felt all the more disappointed that she wasn't there. He was debating whether to call her when he walked into the house where some of the students were already helping themselves to the buffet at the dining room table and saw Ricky standing in the kitchen.

"Hey, buddy." Norman extended his hand. "How are you feeling?"

"Better, so I thought I'd take a ride."

"Would you like something to eat?"

Ricky shook his head. "I'm still a little wobbly. Do you have any ginger ale?"

"Sure." Norman reached down into a cooler of soft drinks and pulled out two cans. "Let's go into my office."

They walked down the hall, past the bedrooms, and into Norman's office. It was a comfortable room with floor-to-ceiling bookshelves, a large window that looked out on the front lawn, a big wooden desk with a computer and printer, and an over-stuffed couch against the wall facing the window. Taking seats at either end of the couch, they flipped open their cans of soda.

"Would you like a glass?"

"No," Ricky assured his friend. "This is fine."

Norman took a sip of his soda. "Whitney Weldon didn't show up today."

Ricky looked puzzled. "She didn't?"

"No. I'm surprised, too. I spoke to her yesterday, and she paid with a credit card. It's a pretty expensive day to just blow off."

"Did you call her?"

"I was going to, but then I figured I'd wait until lunchtime. If she still wasn't here, I'd try her then."

The phone in the office rang.

"I bet that's Dew," Norman said as he got up and walked over to his desk. "She's down at the radio station." He picked up the phone. "Hello. . . . Hi, honey. . . . Yes, everything's fine. . . .

What? . . . The wildfires are spreading, so they're thinking of evacuating? . . . I'd better let the students know. . . . Call me on the cell phone this afternoon if you hear anything more. . . . I'll keep the phone turned on during the session. . . . Talk to you later, babe."

"What's going on?" Ricky asked.

"We haven't gotten enough rain. The trees are so dry, the whole area is like a tinderbox. Wildfires are starting up north, and they're spreading. Homes in the mountains here are the most at risk. The conditions are bad out there, they're just bad. I want to tell the students in case any of them want to leave now."

They left the room in a hurry. Norman did not notice the scribbled message that the maid had left by his computer.

The students were eating their lunch in the large den off the kitchen. Some were on the couches; others were sitting Indian-style on the floor.

"I just received a call from my girlfriend," Norman announced. "She works at the radio station in town. There are wildfires around this whole area, and they're spreading. We might be forced to evacuate."

A collective gasp went up in the room.

"If anyone wants to leave, you can come to the next seminar. I want you to feel comfortable. I would like to stress that they're not evacuating anyone yet. My girlfriend is going to keep me posted. I'll keep my cell phone turned on this afternoon, so we'll hear immediately if things have gotten worse."

Norman's cell phone, which was attached to his belt buckle, rang just then. He picked it up, said hello, and listened. He shook his head several times, then finally hung up.

"Okay, everybody. It's been decided. The fire marshals are being conservative about this. Precautionary. The fires aren't here yet, but they're too close for comfort. We've got to evacuate the area. Time for you all to go home."

"Oh," Adele moaned. "I just knew I was going to have a breakthrough this afternoon."

"Next time, Adele," Norman said dismissively. He turned to Ricky. "Do you want to come down to the radio station with me?"

"Absolutely."

For the moment all thoughts of Whitney were pushed into the background.

46

Charles Bennett had a sleepless night. He'd been watching television and had caught the story on Lucretia's upcoming wedding to that gigolo. It made him sick. It was so obvious that Edward Fields was after her money. So what if he'd given her one piece of good advice when he suggested that she invest in that dot-com. Lucretia had told Charles once, when they were chatting across the fence, that she decided to get out while the getting was good and nobody could talk her out of it. If it had been up to Fields, she would have been left holding the bag like all those other investors who had lost most of their worth.

Lucretia was so cute, he thought. And she's so full of life. Ever since Charles's wife had died five years ago, he'd contented himself with his garden. He had no interest in dating.

"Not at my age," he'd say to anyone who tried to fix him up. Charles remembered how much he'd hated dating when he was a young man. He had worked steadily in the movies from the time he was in his early twenties and often felt that was the main reason many girls wanted to go out with him. When he finally met his wife, he was so relieved that he'd never have to go out on another first date. He knew she was the one. That was fifty-seven years ago, and he'd never dated again!

Charles wanted to ask Lucretia to join him for dinner right after she moved in. They were talking across their backyards when that oily wimp showed up and called her "sweetheart." Charles could tell he was being sent a message and had walked away in disgust. Since then, whenever Lucretia was alone by the pool, he'd made a point of saying hello. If Edward was there, Charles steered clear of that side of his yard.

This morning Charles had gotten out of bed, tired from a lack of sleep, and had gone into town to do some errands, including buying a present for Lucretia's wedding. By the time he got back, a television van was parked in front of Lucretia's house, and the caterers were busily setting up tables in the backyard. The TV cameraman was walking around, recording all the activity. Charles still hadn't decided whether he would attend the wedding or not. The whole thing rubbed him the wrong way. He knew that Lucretia would be in for a bad time. Worse yet, Charles was worried: Who knew what the guy she was marrying was capable of?

Charles wondered what Phyllis thought of the whole thing. She'd been the maid in that house for more than twenty years. Charles certainly didn't know her well, but he'd seen her numerous times over the years when he and his wife were at parties that the previous owners, the Howards, had thrown. Now there was a great couple. Charles laughed. They didn't even mind when Phyllis besieged a game show producer at one of their gatherings, begging him to put her on his show. The producer had a hard time convincing Phyllis that he couldn't use her because he had met her several times, and after the game show scandals of the fifties, the rules were very strict.

Charles made himself a cup of tea and sat down at the dining room table with the newspaper. He read the headlines, but his mind kept wandering back to everything that was going on next door. I know, he finally decided—Lucretia's car isn't there. Maybe I'll just walk over, drop off the wedding present, and see if I can chat Phyllis up a little bit. Get her take on the situation. Not that I can do anything about it, but I'd certainly like to try.

47

Rex hid behind a large oak tree for several minutes, watching the woman he had seen behind the barn. She was walking slowly back through the vineyards toward the house. When he got a good look at her, he realized who she was: the woman in the gift shop! He had stopped in there before the meditation class.

Just what was she doing digging up the land? Probably looking for a bone, he thought. And on her lunch hour, no less. This was definitely not good news. If she found Whitney in the barn, it would all be over.

Twenty-four more hours, he thought. Twenty-four hours and this will be over. Satisfied that there was no one else around, Rex ran for the barn door, hurried inside, and shut the door quickly. He stood still for a moment, his heart pounding. Thumping noises were coming from the corner where the car was. He couldn't believe it. Whitney must be crazy. She was obviously trying to attract attention.

Racing over, Rex opened one of the back doors of her Jeep.

"Stop it," he growled. "You're getting me plenty mad, and you don't want to do that."

Whitney froze.

"I come out here to be a nice guy and bring you some food, and look what you do!"

Whitney's whole body tensed up. She could tell Rex was very nervous, which could be dangerous. She realized that she had better not antagonize him.

"I got you a sandwich for lunch. And as you may or may not know, there's a little toilet in a closet in the corner of the barn. It might not be the most luxurious, but something tells me you'll appreciate it. If you try anything, I will shoot you. Then I'll go and shoot your family. Got it?"

"I don't have to go," Whitney managed to utter spitefully through the gag in her mouth. She couldn't help herself. If he thought he was going to insult her dignity by standing over her while she "used the facilities," he had another think coming. She was just happy that she hadn't had anything to drink before she left the house that morning.

"Well, aren't you the little camel?" he said in an amazed tone. "Feisty, too. I bet you don't want lunch then, either." He threw the bag into the back section of the car. "It's going to be tough to eat when you're all tied up."

Restraining himself from slamming the door of the Jeep, Rex quickly left the barn. Hurrying toward the creek, he decided to take another path back to the house. He'd hike up the mountain and come down much closer to the lodge. If anyone saw him, they'd think he was coming from an entirely different direction.

One thing was certain: He wanted to get as far away from Altered States as possible. Once Eddie arrived, he'd talk to him privately and then hit the road. If the woman from the gift shop discovered Whitney, he'd be in big trouble, and he didn't need any more trouble. Rex was only too familiar with the police and police procedures. He realized that if Whitney was found, he might be incriminated. Even though Whitney had never seen him, there were probably fibers from his clothing in her car. He had to talk to Eddie. And he'd warn him about that Regan Reilly, too. He caught her checking him out today in the meditation class. She was too nosy for her own good.

Rex started sweating as he hiked up the mountain. What had seemed like an easy job was getting messier and messier. Who would have thought that Eddie would be all over national television this weekend? Who could have imagined they'd hire a private detective to try to find Whitney? Who could have predicted that some idiot who worked at the winery would be digging up the area behind the barn where he stashed her?

When Rex reached the top of the mountain, he detected a faint smell of smoke. He had heard that there were wildfires all over the northern hills. He looked down at the barn, which stood alone, far away from the other buildings at Altered States. If fire hit the property, that would be the last building anyone would be concerned about. It was such a junk heap, they'd probably be happy it went up in smoke.

"Sorry about that, Whitney," he muttered under his breath. "It doesn't look like you're going to make it to your Aunt Lucretia's wedding. You may never make it to another wedding. I really wish I could help you out." He turned, vowing never to lay eyes on that barn or Whitney, ever again.

48

———◆———

In the Lower East Side apartment of the recently captured art thief, New York City detectives were gathering evidence. They seized a computer, address book, personal papers, answering machine, and caller ID box. The box held the numbers of the last one hundred calls that were made to that number. A quick scan showed numerous calls from cell phones in the New York area. They were easy to identify because most cell phone users in New York City had a number that began with 917.

The calls that were recorded had all been placed in the last week.

"I can't wait to find out who these numbers belong to," one of the detectives declared.

In a closet the detectives found ski masks, burglar tools, paintings, antique clocks, tapestries, silverware, ceramics, and glassware—all obviously stolen.

"Nice to see he has good taste," one of the investigators muttered.

"Well, isn't this cute!" the detective in charge called out. He pulled a framed picture off a crowded shelf in the living room. The picture had been partially hidden by all the knickknacks and junk that were vying for space.

"What have you got there?" his partner asked.

"A barbershop quartet, except they don't have matching hats and bow ties. It's matching tattoos."

"Holy smoke."

Four guys who did not exactly look like upstanding citizens were holding up their T-shirts. The picture had obviously been taken in a bar after they'd all had more than a few drinks. Every one of them had a tattoo of a skull and crossbones below the navel.

"Sexy, huh? Something tells me these guys are bonded by more than drinking and tattooing."

49

———◆———

This is just so delightful," Nora said admiringly when they walked into the main lodge.

Lilac looked pleased. "Thank you. We love it here."

"Regan tells us you haven't owned the winery for very long."

"No, we haven't," Lilac said as she made her way behind the reception desk.

"I didn't realize how popular this area had become for its wineries," Nora continued.

Lilac laughed. "The outside world is just discovering the wineries of the south central coast. And new vineyards keep springing up all over. The area had a number of wineries operating in the late 1800s and early 1900s that were closed because of Prohibition, this being one of them. It wasn't until 1962 that the first post-Prohibition winery opened in Santa Barbara County."

"The weather is perfect, the scenery is breathtaking, and you're not far from Santa Barbara—or Los Angeles, for that matter. You're close to the ocean, and you have the mountains in your backyard." Nora turned to Luke. "Maybe we should buy a house here."

Luke put his arm around her. "You say that about every place we visit."

"I know."

Regan helped her parents with their bags. Lilac gave them a corner room at the end of the hall that was larger than the one Regan was staying in.

"I guess she knew you guys were coming. My room is a lot smaller."

"We're paying," Luke remarked wryly.

"Well, I wonder what she's saving for Lucretia." Regan sat down on the chaise longue in the corner and looked at her watch. It was only a little after two. "What would you like to do this afternoon?"

"Lilac said she'd love to have us all on the deck out back for a glass of wine at five o'clock. Then dinner," Nora replied. She turned to Luke, who was already stretched out on the bed. "Honey, what do you feel like doing until then?"

"This feels pretty good."

Nora laughed. "I wouldn't mind a little snooze, and then we can take a walk."

"The gift shop is across the way," Regan told them. "And I'm sure Earl would love to meditate with you."

"No thanks," Luke answered hastily.

"I figured that." Regan chuckled. She stood up. "I want to try to reach Whitney. Even though her mother's not concerned, I am. Why don't you relax for a while. I'll be around."

The blast from the engines of twenty-one motorcycles assaulted the peaceful silence of the room. All three of them jumped. "What's that?" Nora cried.

"I don't know!" Regan ran to the door and down the hall, Luke and Nora close behind. Lilac had already run out the front door, practically in a panic. The door was left wide open.

Outside in the parking lot a gang of bikers surrounded a white Rolls-Royce.

"Mom, Dad . . . something tells me Lucretia has arrived."

50

Polly and Sarah liked to go into the center of town in San Luis Obispo on Saturdays. On weekends the town was teeming with students from Cal Poly, as it was known locally, formally called the California Polytechnic State University. San Luis Obispo, twenty miles from the coast, was a charming city nestled among lush rolling hills. Polly and Sarah had grown up in those hills and returned there to "live out their lives in the town where they were born, and where the motel was invented in 1925," as they liked to say.

One might wonder why they liked to go into town on Saturdays when it was so busy. They both felt that it gave them a jolt to see all the kids sipping coffee at the cafes, shopping, hurrying up and down the tree-lined streets of stores and cafes.

"On Saturdays it's most vibrant," they'd say. "That and Thursday nights when we have the Farmers' Market street fair."

They'd checked the computer before breakfast, but so far there was no word from Lucretia.

"Do you think she's just going to ignore us?" Polly asked.

Sarah sipped her coffee and thought about it for a moment. "I don't think so. We just sent the e-mail to the television station last night. Lucretia might not have received it yet. Should we try and call her? She might be listed in the book in Beverly Hills."

"No way! If she doesn't get in touch with us, then too bad about her. And if the TV station wants to come talk to us about the secret, then so be it."

"Polly! You are naughty." Sarah chuckled as she took a bite of one of the homemade blueberry muffins she'd baked the day before. Mine are so much better than the ones Polly makes, she thought. But Polly insisted on baking sometimes and never used a measuring cup. It drove Sarah crazy.

After breakfast they drove into town, Sarah at the wheel. Polly had given up driving. They parked the car, walked around, did their errands, and finally arrived at their favorite cafe for lunch. They were seated outside, at their request, so they could watch all the passersby. It was a beautiful day, not uncommon in their area. They'd generally sit and have lunch, and then linger over a cup of tea, before heading home.

Polly and Sarah had a corner table, right next to an outdoor newsstand. Sarah's seat faced the array of magazines and newspapers on display. One local newspaper was hanging from a hook, front and center. Sarah squinted to get a better focus on the headline.

"What in tarnation?" she asked softly.

"What's the matter?" Polly demanded. "You want to change seats or something?"

"Lord, no." Sarah jumped up. "I'll be right back." Because there was a railing that surrounded the outdoor tables, she had to go back through the restaurant and go out the front door.

As she walked past the tables, Polly called to her, "Where are you going?"

Sarah ignored her. She went over to the newsstand and bought a copy of *Luis Says,* the area's oldest local newspaper. The family paper was now run by Thaddeus Washburne, Jr., the seventy-year-old son of the founder. The front page center headline read: OUR VERY OWN LUCRETIA STANDISH BACK IN THE NEWS.

There was a little picture of Lucretia in the top corner of the front page.

Sarah paid for the paper and hurried back to the table, breathless at the effort. "Will you look at this?" she asked Polly, who had decided to just sit back and wait until Sarah collected herself. She could get so darn excitable sometimes.

"What?"

"There's a story here on Lucretia."

Polly leaned forward. "What does it say?"

Sarah turned the page. "Oh, Lord!"

"What?"

Sarah's mouth was moving as she read the page, but no sound was coming out.

Once again Polly sat back. We'll get to it, she thought, in what Polly had dubbed "Sarah's time."

Sarah shook her head and turned the page again.

"Oh, Lord!"

"What?"

"There's a picture of the three of us taken when we danced in that festival on the beach."

"Give me that." Polly grabbed the paper from Sarah's hands. The picture of Lucretia, Polly, and Sarah kicking their legs up was in the center of the page with the caption "Lucretia Standish with two unidentified chums as they danced at the Festival by the Beach. Circa 1919."

"Unidentified?" Polly snapped. "How could they not know our names?"

"And where did they get that picture? I don't think I've ever seen it."

Polly started to read the article.

"It doesn't say anything new," Sarah said quickly. "Let's get our check and stop at the newspaper office. We may as well let them know who we are so they can run a correction."

"You're darn tootin'."

51

Frank and Heidi were having a bad day. They'd visited two other potential investors, and only one of them had coughed up a check. It was for a measly thousand dollars.

"That won't even pay our doughnut bill," Heidi complained. "We're up the river, Kipsman, and we're without a paddle."

They were heading north on 101, on their way to Altered States.

Frank couldn't believe they were going to the winery that Whitney's family owned. He didn't dare mention that to Heidi. He realized that meant Lucretia Standish was related to Whitney. Maybe she'd be willing to invest in the movie because Whitney had such a good role.

Two things were bothering Frank. Would it embarrass Whitney if representatives from the movie she was working on showed up looking for money from one of her relatives? The other, more important matter was that she still hadn't called back. Where was she? Frank couldn't have answered her call in front of Heidi, but he had checked his phone a number of times. Whitney hadn't even tried to reach him. Was she angry with him about something? What if she had gone to the winery?

"It's a good script, don't you think?" Heidi asked Frank, looking for reassurance.

"It's a great script. And I think the movie has a real shot." He hesitated. I have to tell her that we're on our way to Whitney's family winery, he thought, because sometimes Heidi exaggerates in her spiel about the film. Not lies; she just blows around a lot of hot air. She'd end up looking like a fool when it comes out that Whitney is related to these people. And of course it would come out. It would be better if Heidi were prepared. She could lay it on about how talented Whitney was, how good she was in the movie, and how important the film was for her career—all of which was true. "What did you say the name of that winery was?" Frank asked.

Heidi looked at her notes. "Altered States."

"You know," he said slowly, "that name sounds so familiar. Where did I hear it before? Hmmmm. . . . I know. . . . That's the winery owned by Whitney Weldon's family."

"What? Her family owns a winery?" Heidi eyed Frank suspiciously. Then she glanced down at her notes. "Wait a minute! Lucretia Standish said she was going to her niece and nephews' winery. That means they're related." Heidi broke into a huge smile. "It might make it easier to get Lucretia to agree to invest."

"Let's hope." Frank turned on the radio. He had a feeling that Whitney was in trouble. Well, I guess I'll find out soon enough.

"When did Whitney tell you her family owned a winery?" Heidi drilled him.

Here we go, Frank thought. He wished he could find someone else for Heidi to nag. In her own way Heidi was a good producer for him to work with. If only he could get her away from any thoughts of romance. "At the first audition," he answered.

"How did it come up?" Heidi pressed.

Frank sighed. "I told her Whitney Weldon was a good name for an actress. She laughed and said, 'What about Freshness Weldon?' "

Heidi made a face. "Freshness Weldon?"

"Her mother was a hippie. That's what Whitney was named when she was born, because the air was so fresh that day. Whitney then added that her family had a winery which her mother had dubbed 'Altered States.' " Frank laughed. "She was pretty funny when she was telling the story."

"How cute," Heidi said curtly. "Funny the name Altered States didn't ring a bell before. You certainly remember Whitney's story very well." She pulled out her cell phone. "I have to call my assistant."

That's a relief. No one would ever call you Freshness, he thought. Whitney is Freshness. That's what I'll have to call her from now on. She'll just laugh in that endearing way of hers.

He couldn't wait to see her again.

52

"Will you look at that?" Nora whispered as they witnessed Lucretia stepping out of the car like the grand movie star she used to be, waving at the growing crowd of gawkers.

Earl had been conducting a meditation class when the motorcycles pulled up. Needless to say, the peace and calm in the studio evaporated. Earl's words about meditation being the path to enlightenment were forgotten as his students jumped up from their mats and bolted from the room.

"Calm, calm, calm," Earl instructed to no avail. "If you can't beat 'em, join 'em," he then muttered under his breath as he, too, ran to find the source of the commotion. A moment later they were all outside, gazing in amazement at the sight of the Road's Scholars. A camera crew was shooting everything: the motorcyclists, Lucretia getting out of the Rolls, and the reactions of the people emerging from the tasting room and the meditation center.

"There's the future Mr. Lucretia Standish," Regan noted as Edward Fields exited the Rolls wearing a pair of dark glasses that covered half his face. He looked like someone on his way home from the plastic surgeon's after an eye job, someone who clearly didn't want to be recognized. "Let's go outside," Regan said to her parents.

Lilac, Earl, and Leon were standing together, respectfully greeting their long-lost or never-met aunt Lucretia. Their soon-to-be Uncle Edward stood back like a true prince consort. The motorcyclists had gotten off their bikes and taken off their helmets, as if they planned to stay. Regan thought that a few of them were actually preening for the camera.

"What a scene," Regan whispered to her parents as Lilac called them over.

Lilac made the introductions: "Meet Lucretia and Edward."

Nora and Luke shook hands with Lucretia.

"Nora Regan Reilly, the writer? I've read all your books!" Lucretia exclaimed.

"Thank you."

"And this is Regan Reilly," Lilac said. "She's a private investigator. We called her to help us find Whitney, who went off for the weekend before she knew about your wedding."

"Did you find her?" Lucretia asked excitedly.

"She came home unexpectedly last night. Today she went to an acting seminar, but she'll be here tomorrow."

"Marvelous! I can't wait to talk to her about her work."

Regan instinctively liked Lucretia. She seemed like a fragile little bird with boundless energy. When Regan shook Edward's hand, not surprisingly she felt an instant dislike for him. His palm was sweaty, his handshake weak, and he seemed aloof. "Nice to meet you. Edward is your name?" she asked.

"Yes," he answered, looking past her.

I hate when people do that, Regan thought as she turned to see what had captured his attention. Emerging from the vineyard was Don, her neighbor from the meditation class. His skull and crossbones tattoo can't compare to the ones on the motorcycle gang, Regan thought.

"These nice boys escorted us up here." Lucretia gestured at

the group. "And tomorrow they're coming to the wedding. Dirt, here, gave me a ride on his bike when we met them at the restaurant on the way here."

"How nice of them," Leon said guardedly. He wasn't sure he wanted a group like this on his property.

"How about a glass of our wine for everyone?" Lilac called out so they all could hear.

"We don't drink and drive," Dirt pronounced. He was clearly their leader. "It's hard to have a designated driver when you're all on motorcycles, you know." He pointed his two forefingers. "We only drink when we've arrived where we're staying for the night."

"Where are you staying tonight?" Lilac asked.

"We don't know yet. We have our bedrolls. We'll see."

"Stay here," Lucretia cried. "We'll have such a good time. Then we can all ride down to the wedding in the morning in style."

"I'd love it if you stayed," Lilac said hesitantly. "But we don't have enough bedrooms."

"We sleep under the stars," Dirt said. "On these weekends we just take it as it comes."

"My daughter enjoys go-with-the-flow weekends," Lilac said enthusiastically.

"Not anymore," Leon muttered.

"What did you say?" Lucretia asked him.

"Nothing. It's just that we worry about Whitney when she disappears and we can't get in touch."

Especially when there are millions of dollars at stake, Regan thought.

"You're welcome to stay here tonight and sleep under our stars," Lilac offered. "Roam around, enjoy, have dinner with us."

"We don't want to put you to any trouble," Dirt said. "The big thing is, we just wanted to make sure this little lady Lucretia arrived safe and sound. We don't want anything to happen to her," he said, training his gaze on Edward and baring his teeth in a warning smile.

Interesting, Regan thought. These guys have Edward's story. She watched as Edward wiped his brow and attempted a smile.

Leon could tell that Lucretia was enjoying the motorcycle gang. And God knows we want to make her happy, he thought. "We'd love to have you stay," he finally said with an air of authority. "It's no trouble at all."

Dirt leaned against his bike, crossed his arms, and looked as if he were mulling it over. All the while the camera was recording him. He milked the attention for all it was worth. Dirt turned to his group. None of them moved a muscle. He turned back. "We accept your offer. But only if we can go out and bring back food for dinner. You got a grill?"

"A big one on our deck," Lilac said proudly.

"Good. We'll bring back burgers and hot dogs and maybe some corn on the cob, potato salad, stuff like that. Then we'll sample your wine."

Lucretia jumped up and down. "Isn't this fun, Edward? We're having a real rehearsal dinner."

Edward managed another feeble smile.

Regan got the distinct feeling that Edward wasn't having nearly as much fun as Lucretia. He must hate us all, she thought. He just wants to marry her, get her money, and get it over with.

Dirt cleared his throat. "Lucretia told me she's meeting you folks for the first time, so we'll get out of here and give you some time alone, ya know, some quality family time while we check out the countryside and do some food shopping. We'll be back about six o'clock, and then we'll fire up the barbecue. And we'll make toasts to the happy couple. How does that sound?"

"Wonderful," Lilac answered. "Do you think you could pick up some turkey burgers?"

"No problem."

As the guys started to get back on their bikes and Lucretia started to chatter about how happy she was, one of the bikers walked up to Edward. Regan overheard him asking Edward if he would like anything special for dinner. "You seem like the type who likes chicken," the biker said to him in an odd way.

"A ha-ha-hamburger would be fine," Edward stammered.

"A hamburger it is then," the tattooed hulk repeated and then walked away.

That was strange, Regan thought. This is all so strange. What was going to be an intimate family evening at Altered States has now turned into a barbecue with a motorcycle gang who will be sleeping outside our windows. But that didn't bother Regan. All she cared about was determining that Whitney was okay. She hadn't called back, and that was a worry.

As the motorcyclists disappeared down the road, kicking up a dust storm, and the meditators and wine tasters returned to their previous business, the rest of the group started to walk into the lodge.

Lilac turned to the camera crew. "Would you like to come inside?"

"Right now we'll walk around and get some shots of the winery if you don't mind," the assistant to the cameraman said. "Then we'll be on our way."

"Come with me," Leon said proudly. "I'll show you my machines. You can see how we turn out our beautiful wine."

Who else is going to turn up? Regan wondered.

Then something else happened that seemed strange to her.

Edward was getting the bags out of the car when Don Lesser appeared from the shadows and offered him a hand. She didn't know why, but it just seemed odd.

Let me go in and call Whitney, she thought. And of course I'd really like to talk to Jack.

53

Bella was freaking out. She overheard everything that was discussed in the parking lot with that gang of weirdos. They were going to spend the night at Altered States! What if they started roaming around the property and discovered the holes in the ground and the piles of dirt behind the barn? She'd be found out. Or Lilac and her brothers might start digging themselves and discover Grandpa Ward's treasure. Bella couldn't let it happen.

What if that pack wanted to sleep "under the stars" back there?

Bella had gotten the lay of the land in the week she'd been working at Altered States. Earl was on a continual cloud in the meditation center, Lilac spent her days fussing over the gift shop and bed-and-breakfast in the main lodge, and Leon rarely emerged from the winery building. He spent the day with his stainless steel tanks, his oak barrels, his crushers and pressers and vats, and whatever other gizmos were used in the process of producing a bottle of wine.

None of the Weldons had any interest in wandering over to the barn. Bella was reasonably sure of that. But now these bikers . . .

A woman and her teenage daughter were puttering around the gift shop. Bella had poured wine for two couples who had taken their glasses outside to the picnic tables. She wished everyone would leave. She was aching to run out of there and get back to the grounds behind the barn. She decided to call Walter and tell him to get his sorry behind over to the winery and start digging. Too bad about his back. *He'll be able to afford a massage every day if we find a pot of gold.*

There was a phone on the counter that Bella could use for local calls, but she was afraid someone would overhear her conversation. As soon as the coast was clear, she'd make a quick call. *If only these people would get out of here.*

Finally the woman approached the register with a dozen candles in her hands. "Do you get those motorcycle types around here all the time?" she asked as Bella started to ring up the purchases.

"Oh, I don't think so," Bella said. "But I just started working here this week."

"You don't say."

"I do." Bella quickly gave the woman her change and placed the candles in a gift box. She wanted to hurry the customers out of there. She was dying to call Walter.

"It's so pretty here. We just drove up from Los Angeles. They say on the radio there are wildfires springing up all over the place. I hope they don't do too much damage."

"It's been a dry spring," Bella acknowledged, "which makes it dangerous." *Now please leave,* she thought.

The woman clearly wasn't finished chatting. As she fumbled in her purse for her keys, she continued, "They were interviewing a guy on the radio who lives up in Oceanview. They had to evacuate a school where they were holding Saturday classes."

The daughter, who hadn't made a sound, suddenly piped up: "The students must have been glad."

"Oh, but dear, we're talking about fires here. That's nothing to joke about."

The girl shrugged.

Get out, Bella was screaming inside. Just get out of here. If the fire reaches this property, I'll never find my treasure.

"Did you get all the candles you wanted?" the woman asked her daughter.

The girl nodded.

"Well, bye now."

"Good-bye," Bella practically snarled. She picked up the phone and quickly dialed her home number.

"Walter!" she cried when he answered.

Walter was stretched out on the couch in their little rental apartment. "Yeah. Hi, honey."

"Get off the couch."

"How do you know I'm on the couch?"

"I'm psychic. Listen, you have to start digging behind the barn now."

"What?"

"You have to."

"Why?"

"Because we don't have much time. A gang of motorcyclists is staying on the property tonight, the wildfires are spreading, a camera crew is snooping around, and there seems to be a million reasons why that treasure might slip out of our hands."

Walter had the ball game on. "But my back hurts."

"Walter!"

Walter knew he had no choice, as usual. "Oh, all right," he agreed. Bella had pointed out the road that led to the old barn, so he knew exactly where to go.

"Go buy another shovel. I'll join you as soon as I finish up here. I expect you to have moved a lot of earth by then." Just then a man walked into the gift shop. She'd seen him coming from the fields when they were all outside greeting Lucretia.

"Okay, sweetie pie," Bella said cheerfully. "I'll see you later." She hung up the phone. "Can I help you with anything?"

"I'd like to taste some wine. May I sit at the table over there?"

"Certainly," she said agreeably, happy now that she'd called Walter into action.

A moment later the groom-to-be also walked in.

"Hello there," Bella greeted Edward. "Congratulations to you."

"Thank you," he answered nervously. "How did you know?"

"I saw you outside!"

Edward looked around. "I just want to buy her a present," he confided.

"How about a taste of wine first?" Bella suggested.

"That sounds great."

"Have a seat," Bella encouraged as she prepared two glasses.

The two men sat at the long table. Bella couldn't possibly imagine that they were there not only to talk to each other but also to check her out.

"My grandfather used to own this winery," she volunteered as she poured wine for them. She looked up when she heard someone walk in. "Hello, Regan," Bella called. "Are you going to have some wine, too?"

"No, thanks," Regan responded, taking in the sight of Don and Edward at the table, conversing with Bella. A sign on the wall over the table read IN VINO VERITAS.

In wine there is truth, Regan translated. And wouldn't I love to know the truth about those three. All of them seemed suspicious. Just what was going on?

54

Charles Bennett peeked outside to make sure the television van was gone. Seeing that the coast was clear, he left his house and walked across the lawn to Lucretia's, wedding gift in hand. He had chosen a set of wineglasses from Tiffany's for the bride and groom.

Reaching the front steps, he rang Lucretia's bell and waited. This house is so lovely, and in all the years I've lived next door, good people have always occupied this abode, he reflected. That was about to change with Edward Fields moving in.

"Coming," a voice called from inside the house. Two seconds later Phyllis opened the door. "Mr. Bennett, what a nice surprise."

"I thought I'd drop off Lucretia's present."

"Please come in."

Charles hadn't been inside the house since Lucretia had bought it. "As I recall, this looks exactly the same way it did when I was at a party here a couple of years ago," he observed.

"Lucretia took everything as is," Phyllis affirmed. "Same furniture, same paintings, same maid. I was just making a cup of tea. Would you like one?"

"I'd love one," he said, glad that they'd have a chance to talk. Phyllis looked a little strained to him.

Glancing out the window in the kitchen, Charles noticed all the tables that had been set up for the wedding reception. "I see you're getting everything ready for the big day," he commented in a less than enthusiastic tone.

"Uh-huh." Phyllis poured boiling water into a china teapot. "We've had a bit of excitement around here this morning."

"I saw the television piece last night."

"Apparently a lot of people were watching. It's caused quite a stir."

Charles looked at her quizzically. "What happened?"

"In the middle of the night Lucretia received a number of phone calls from angry viewers. They're still coming in. This morning she found tomatoes all over the front steps. Talk about bruised fruit. So she got out of town."

"Where did she go?"

"Lucretia's niece called this morning. She and her two brothers own a winery near Santa Barbara. They invited Lucretia and Edward to visit for the day and stay there tonight. They're going to have a big dinner. Lucretia was gone already when the reporter showed up again. Lucretia called while the reporter was here because she happened to catch the follow-up report they did today. She and Edward were having lunch in a diner when the story was being broadcast. So now the reporter is headed to the winery, too."

"Why?"

"Because, as only Lucretia can, she ended up with a twenty-one-man motorcycle escort to the winery."

Charles laughed heartily. "I don't know her well, but that sounds like Lucretia to me." He sat at one of the stools next to the counter and suddenly felt sad. Lucretia was going to marry someone who probably couldn't care less about her. "I don't like this guy!" he blurted out unexpectedly.

Phyllis, who had been reaching for the teacups in the cabinet, turned to him quickly. "I can't stand him."

"What are we going to do?" Charles wondered aloud.

Phyllis exhaled deeply. "Nothing we can do at this point." She looked him straight in the eye. "Do you have a crush on Lucretia or something?"

"I certainly do."

They both laughed.

"You know, Phyllis, if you can't say what you feel at my age, then when can you say it? As soon as Lucretia moved in and I realized who she was, I got so excited. It's not often I meet someone I can reminisce with anymore. We were both actors in the good old days. I was never in a silent film and she was never in a talkie, but it doesn't matter. We'd understand each other. We could have a good time together."

This man is so nice, Phyllis thought. If he finds out that I lied to Lilac so that I'd get some of Lucretia's money, he'd never forgive me.

The phone rang. "Get ready for this," Phyllis said to Charles as she put on the speakerphone. "Hello. Standish residence."

"Drop dead! I hope Lucretia chokes on her wedding cake!"

"I'll give her the message," Phyllis replied, promptly disconnecting the caller.

Charles laughed again. "I didn't know you had such a sense of humor."

"Being a maid all these years, with the things I've had to put up with, you have to see the humor in these situations."

"That call worries me, though."

"Lucretia's going to get an unlisted number," Phyllis assured him. "But right now this phone is all we've got." She poured the tea into their cups.

"I don't like the fact that Lucretia is a target for all the crazy people out there watching television. I wish I could just bring her back and protect her." Charles crossed his arms and sighed.

"You've got it worse than I thought," Phyllis teased with a raised eyebrow.

"Seriously, Phyllis, we have to put our heads together and get rid of this guy!"

Just as long as I get my money, Phyllis thought. Just as long as I get my money.

55

The office of the local weekly, *Luis Says,* was located in a white stone cottage on a quiet street in San Luis Obispo. Inside, Thaddeus Washburne was alone at his desk. He always came in for a couple of hours on Saturday because he loved his work. The newspaper had been in the Washburne family for so long that it felt like an actual family member—a family member that needed as much care and attention as any relative, and probably more. Other men played golf on weekends. Thaddeus went into the office and poked around his files. Now that his wife was gone, he spent even more time there than usual.

The paper went to press late Friday night. Thaddeus was still in the office when GOS News did the first story on Lucretia Standish. Moving fast, Thaddeus wrote his own story about Lucretia for the paper that was within hours of being published. The Washburne family had always had a particular interest in covering human interest stories about people who had grown up in the area and then gone on to become famous. Thaddeus's father had started a file on Lucretia when she was making movies. Thaddeus dug out the file for background information and used the old pictures in it for his story.

Lucretia's life was quite a tale. He wanted to run another, more detailed article, but he was sure it would be hard to get hold of her personally. He kept the television on in the corner of the office and followed the continuing coverage of Lucretia's adventures. GOS was running the story every hour, it seemed. Thaddeus had watched Lucretia's maid on a segment that morning. He couldn't believe Lucretia had made all that money off a dot-com.

The doorbell rang. Who could be visiting here on a Saturday? he wondered as he pushed himself out of his chair. He opened the door and was surprised to find two elderly ladies standing outside.

"May I help you?" he asked.

"We have something we had to get off our chests." Sarah held up the latest edition of *Luis Says*. "We're Lucretia Standish's 'unidentified chums.' "

Thaddeus broke into a hearty laugh. "I love it! Please come in, won't you?"

They followed him into the comfortable one-room cottage. The Washburnes had knocked down the walls years ago so that all the employees could be within shouting distance of one another, like the bull pen of a big-city daily. Even though it was a small room and it was a small local paper, they felt it gave them a certain big-city spirit.

Thaddeus pulled two chairs up to his desk. "By the way, I'm Thaddeus Washburne." He extended his hand.

Sarah, always the leader, shook his hand first. "I'm Sarah Desmond."

"And I'm Polly Cook. We can give you the spellings of our names for the next time you use our picture."

Thaddeus laughed again. "May I get you a cup of coffee?"

"Water would be fine," Sarah answered.

Polly nodded. "Water would be good. I could drink coffee and tea all day long, but then I don't sleep at night."

"Ever try decaf?" Thaddeus asked.

Polly grimaced. "Don't like the taste."

"We try to drink eight glasses of water a day," Sarah informed him. "It's a chore, let me tell you."

"Gives me a bloated feeling," Polly agreed.

"You gals must be doing something right," Thaddeus noted. "You certainly don't look your age. If you didn't tell me you were ninety-three-year-old Lucretia Standish's friends from childhood, I'd have guessed your ages to be at least fifteen years younger."

Polly and Sarah smiled coyly at Thaddeus and then slyly at each other as Thaddeus went off to fetch their refreshments.

Thaddeus grabbed two glasses in the kitchenette and filled them from a watercooler that emitted a loud gurgle as he walked back to his desk. At that moment the GOS anchor announced that Lucretia Standish was "having quite a weekend."

Polly and Sarah both gasped, then shushed each other. Thaddeus put the glasses down on his desk, grabbed the remote control, and turned up the volume. A shot of the sign for Altered States Winery filled the screen. Suddenly a tough motorcyclist rode past the sign, followed by a white Rolls-Royce and then a large cluster of bikers riding in formation.

"Lucretia Standish went to visit her relatives at their winery where a rehearsal dinner will be held tonight. She had a motorcycle escort from a group called the Road's Scholars."

The next shot was of Lucretia getting out of the car, waving regally to the crowd, and smiling for the camera.

"Oh my goodness," Polly declared. "Will you look at that?"

"Jealous?" Sarah asked.

Polly raised her right eyebrow. "Maybe."

" . . . Lucretia and her fiancé greeted her family."

"He is a youngster," Thaddeus observed, almost to himself.

"How can you tell with those glasses?" Sarah snorted. She leaned closer to the television. "Isn't that Nora Regan Reilly?"

Lucretia was shaking hands with several people.

"I think it is," Polly agreed. "Remember we heard her speak at Cal Poly a couple of years back?"

"Sure do."

"We covered her lecture in our paper. That definitely is Nora Regan Reilly," Thaddeus assured them. "I remember how pretty she was and how tall her husband was. He's standing there right next to her."

"He's a nice man. We both read her books," Sarah said. "I wonder what she's doing there."

" . . . We'll be bringing you more updates about Lucretia Standish's wedding weekend later in the day. If you have any comments, please e-mail us at—"

Thaddeus lowered the volume. "Good Lord. Where did Lucretia find those motorcycle guys?"

"She always liked to have fun," Sarah remarked, her head moving slowly from side to side.

"We had the best times with her, just the best," Polly added. "She was a daredevil. Never scared of anything."

"From the way you talk, I guess you don't see her anymore."

"Haven't since before any of us married. We lost touch when her career faltered and she left California. It's funny to see her getting married again. We had all made a pact that we'd be each other's bridesmaids." Polly stared wistfully at the television screen.

"I'd love to do a story on the three of you," Thaddeus said thoughtfully "Have you two always lived here?"

"Oh, no. We both married and moved away. I ended up in San Francisco and Polly in San Diego. When our husbands died, we decided to live together. Since neither one of us wanted to move to the other's city, we compromised and moved back here where we both feel comfortable. We're not far from our families—just a day's drive at the most."

"We cover the coastline of California in our travels. When we go out to the highway, sometimes we turn right and sometimes we turn left," Polly explained.

"Uh-huh. It would be great to get the three of you together again after all these years. We can invite Lucretia back here for one of the summer festivals. It'd make a great story. Why don't you try to get in touch with her?"

"We already did!" Sarah declared. "We sent an e-mail to that news station and included a private message to Lucretia. But we haven't heard back from her."

"We just sent it last night, and we haven't been home all day," Polly reminded Sarah. "Maybe when we get home there will be a reply."

"What's your Internet server?" Thaddeus asked quickly.

"Pluto," Sarah answered.

"I have the same one! Use my computer to check your e-mail."

Polly, who was even more of an Internet junkie than Sarah, jumped up and came around behind the desk. Thaddeus got up, and Polly quickly took his seat.

"Nice chair."

"Thanks."

Polly typed in her password as they all remained silent. She clicked again, and her e-mails popped up. "Lucretia wrote back!" she cried.

Sarah, Polly, and Thaddeus leaned toward the computer as Polly clicked on Lucretia's e-mail.

Dear Sarah and Polly,

How wonderful to hear from you! It's been too long. I'd love it if you came to the wedding, but I don't know where you are. If you get this and don't live too far away, please be at my house in Beverly Hills on Sunday morning at eleven. You can be my bridesmaids! Remember our pact? Speaking of pacts, PLEASE PLEASE PLEASE keep your lips sealed about our secret. Bring dates if you like. The more the merrier! I'll type my address and phone number at the bottom. Right now I'm away, but I hope to see you tomorrow.

Love,

Lukey

P.S. I wish we could have one of our graveyard chats tonight!

"That must be some secret," Thaddeus said eagerly, clearly hoping to be let in on the intrigue.

Polly and Sarah both giggled. "We can't tell," Sarah declared.

"After all, she invited us to her wedding," Polly added.

"Are you going to go?" Thaddeus asked.

"Of course!" Sarah responded without even looking at Polly. "Do you want to be our date?" she asked after a moment. She could sense he was feeling left out.

Thaddeus's face beamed. "I'd love to accompany you lovely ladies," he replied. "I'll bring my camera and take a current picture of the three of you. Heck, we'll do a special edition! That is if Lucretia doesn't charge me millions for the rights."

"She's already got millions."

"You know," Polly remarked, "rehearsal dinners are always a lot more fun than weddings—at least in my experience."

"But we're not invited."

"Bridesmaids are always invited to the rehearsal dinners." Polly turned to Thaddeus. "What was the name of that winery? Altered something? Where is it?"

"Altered States. Let's see if we can find it." Thaddeus leaned down and started typing. He was a whiz at getting information not only from his interviewees, but also from the computer. "Altered States is not that far from here at all. I'd say an hour's drive at the most."

Polly and Sarah looked at each other. "Isn't it kind of pushy to just show up?" Sarah asked in an unsure tone.

"She'd invite us if she knew we were so close by. We can say we just wanted to drop by to make a toast."

"She said she wanted to have a graveyard chat with you two," Thaddeus offered encouragingly. "Maybe you can have that chat after all."

"Let's do it," Sarah urged. "At this age what have we got to lose?"

Thaddeus shook his head. "Ninety-three. Unbelievable."

"Whatever," Sarah said. "Are you driving us, Mr. Washburne?"

"Absolutely. It'd be my pleasure."

56

When Regan left the gift shop, she was not filled with good vibes. Edward was obviously not a model groom. Bella had a few screws loose, and that Don character was beyond strange. Regan was sure that Edward and Don were connected somehow. She thought a moment. But then again, Edward and Lucretia only decided to come up here today. Don had arrived last night. They couldn't have planned it because Lilac was the one who suggested that Edward and Lucretia pay a little visit.

Regan shrugged and started to walk across the parking lot to the main lodge. She still hadn't called Whitney or Jack. Without knowing quite why, she suddenly turned around and walked back into the gift shop.

"On second thought I think I will take a taste of wine," she told Bella, who didn't look nearly as startled at Regan's reappearance as the two guys.

"Great," Bella said. "Have a seat at our tasting table. Would you like red or white?"

"Red." Regan sat down on the bench next to Edward. "Hello again," she murmured as Bella poured from the Weldon Estate bottle into Regan's glass. Was that dirt under her fingernails?

Regan wondered with surprise. She hadn't noticed it this morning. Bella was so exact about her makeup. Anyone who takes the trouble to line her lips the way she does would definitely keep her nails clean. Her nails were a little chipped, too. She finished pouring and put down the bottle.

"Hope you like it."

Regan lifted her glass and held it out. "Cheers," she trilled lightly to Edward and Don.

They both mumbled "cheers" and sipped.

"If you need anything, I'll be over at the register," Bella announced and scurried off.

A lively crowd, Regan thought. She held up her glass again. "Edward, to your wedding."

"Thank you." Edward sipped from his glass.

"You must be so excited," Regan said. "Are you from Beverly Hills?"

"No."

"Where are you from then?"

"New York."

"Really. What part?" Regan enjoyed watching him squirm.

"Originally Long Island." He cleared his throat. "But I've lived in Manhattan."

"How about you, Don?"

He was staring out the window.

"Don?" Regan repeated.

"Oh," he said abruptly, turning his head.

That was weird, Regan thought. "Where are you from?"

"All over."

The two fountains of information suddenly decided that they had things to do. Draining their glasses, they both got up.

"I've got to check on Lucretia," Edward explained to Regan.

"I'm going to be hitting the road soon," Don said.

"You're leaving?" Regan asked.

He nodded. "I'm meeting some friends." The look on his face told Regan that her questions were not at all welcome. But she already knew that.

"Whatever you do, have fun," Regan urged him. Well, at least I rattled them, she thought as they both left the tasting room. I want to get Don's license number before he takes off for parts unknown, Regan thought. She waited a couple of minutes, then went out to the parking lot. She knew that Don was driving a dark SUV. There was only one SUV in the driveway at the moment. Regan walked over and cautiously circled it. She noticed rental papers on the front seat. Interesting. He would've needed to produce a driver's license to rent the car. Regan knew that information would be on record and could be produced if need be.

The license plate on the back of the car was from the State of California. Regan memorized it and hurried inside the lodge. She went to her room and wrote the number down in her notebook. Satisfied that she had at least accomplished something, she picked up her cell phone and dialed Whitney's number. Once again it was answered by the voice mail.

"Whitney, this is Regan Reilly. If you get this message, please call my cell phone." Regan gave the number. "Thanks so much. I hope your seminar is going well." As Regan hung up the phone, she couldn't help but feel that her last words hung heavily in the air, just as when you tell someone who's really sick how great they look. You want so much for it to be true. Quickly she dialed the number of the seminar that she had in her notebook. Another voice mail picked up. "Hello, this is Norman and Dew. We're not here right now . . ."

I guess Dew's parents were hippies, too, Regan thought. "Hi, my name is Regan Reilly," she said at the sound of the tone and left a message for Whitney Weldon to please call her.

Finally, she called Jack. Thank God he answered. "Hi there. What's going on?" Regan asked.

"What a day. We've had some great breaks with this group of art thieves. I think we're going to nail them, although there's one who's been really elusive. He's wanted in several states and always manages to slip through the cracks. How was your day?"

"Well, Lucretia arrived with a gang of motorcyclists."

Jack laughed. "Are you kidding?"

"I'm not. They're coming back to actually cook what is now being called the rehearsal dinner. You should see these guys! It's kind of cute. They want to protect Lucretia."

"It sounds as if she could use it."

"They're a bunch of characters. Let me tell you this—I would definitely want them on my side. Most of them are very big. And I've never seen so many tattoos in my life."

"Tattoos?" Jack said. "That's funny. The gang we're looking into has a fondness for tattoos as well."

"They do?"

"One of my detectives found a picture in the apartment we searched. It shows four of the crew with skull and crossbones tattoos under their navel."

Regan gripped the phone tighter in her hand. "You're kidding me."

"No. Regan, what's wrong?"

Regan lowered her voice. "There's a guy staying at the bed-and-breakfast here who has a skull and crossbones tattoo under his navel. I already have my suspicions that he's up to no good."

"Regan, these guys are dangerous," Jack cautioned, unable to keep the alarm out of his voice. "Now tell me whatever you know about him."

57

Once all the attendees at Norman's seminar were out the door, he hurried back to his office and unlocked the file cabinet. The bottom drawer was where he and Dew kept their important documents: passports, birth certificates, Norman's divorce decree (his most prized possession), insurance policies, the title to the house, his checkbook, and various other papers he hadn't looked at in ages. He threw everything into a gym bag and then ran into the bedroom and grabbed the only copy of the screenplay he'd recently completed. It was the script he'd written with Whitney Weldon in mind. Her call yesterday had prompted him to reread the script—he definitely thought it was his best work.

Norman raced down the hall and hurried to the back of the house. He turned on the alarm, stepped outside, and locked the door. "I hope that's worth doing," he mused. "A burned-down house has no need for protection from burglars."

Ricky was waiting in his own car, ready to follow Norman to the radio station. Norman backed down the driveway, pulled past Ricky's VW bug, and waved.

They drove down the winding mountain roads, headed for the little town of Calimook, five miles away. Smoke was billowing eerily from the treetops in the distance.

Fifteen minutes later they arrived at the small local radio

station where Dew worked as a disc jockey. She enjoyed bantering with the guests on her show and keeping her listeners up-to-date with all the latest news and activities in Calimook and beyond. She also played an occasional song. Her favorite group was the Beach Boys. Norman had grown up with the Wilson Brothers, and he passed his fondness for the group on to her.

Dew had developed a loyal and growing following, and the owners of the mom-and-pop operation let her do as she pleased. This afternoon she was giving constant updates about the wildfires. The fires were popping up all over; some were small enough to be extinguished quickly, but others were burning out of control. Dew reported the first evacuation in the area and promised to relay any further evacuation plans as soon as the station had any new information.

A commercial break was just starting when Dew looked through the window of her broadcast booth and saw Norman and their friend Ricky in the reception area. She took off her headphones, pushed back her chair, and hurried outside to greet them. Pretty, with long, curly light brown hair, a sprinkling of freckles across her nose and cheeks, and deep blue eyes, Dew was the quintessential California beach girl. Her wardrobe consisted of jeans and countless funky tops. Getting dressed up was not one of her priorities.

"Hi, honey," she greeted Norman, giving him a quick kiss. She could tell he was worried. "Ricky, it's good to see you," she continued as she gave her childhood friend a quick hug.

"I had just stopped up at the house when you called," Ricky explained.

"Dew," the engineer called. "This is a short break. You're going back on in a minute."

Dew grabbed Norman's arm. "Why don't you two come on the air with me?"

"Why?"

"For *Dialogue with Dew*. We can talk about having to evacuate."

"Hurry, Dew!" the engineer called again.

Norman and Ricky followed Dew back into the broadcast room and sat across from her in two leather chairs that had microphones in front of them. Dew winked as the commercial wound down and they were back on the air.

"You are back with Dew," she chimed into the microphone. "And right now I have a couple of guests for a *Dialogue with Dew* session. As many of you know, my boyfriend is Norman Broda. We live in a house up on the mountain in the area they evacuated. Norman is here with me right now, and so is a friend of ours, Ricky Ortiz, who has been working as a production assistant on a movie near Santa Barbara. Who's in the movie, Ricky?" Dew asked quickly.

"An actress named Whitney Weldon is the star. She's not a household name yet but has done a lot of good work."

"Oh, yes, Whitney Weldon. I've seen her in a few movies. Hey, everybody out there. Norman runs these terrific acting workshops up at our house. Whitney Weldon had signed up for the seminar that took place today. Was she there?" Dew asked Norman with a smile.

Norman hesitated for a moment. "No, she didn't make it."

"Oh, she didn't," Dew said, trying to sound upbeat. "She probably heard about the wildfires . . ."

"We had to cancel the rest of today's session when you called me about the evacuation," Norman told Dew. "So it was better for Whitney. She's welcome to attend the next workshop."

"She's so funny in this movie," Ricky interjected. "Really funny."

"What's the name of the movie?" Dew asked Ricky.

"Jinxed."

58

Regan walked over to the window in her room and shut the sliding glass door. She didn't want there to be any chance she'd be overheard.

"He said his name is Don Lesser. I called him Don before, and he didn't answer immediately. It seemed as if he wasn't used to that name."

"So many of this group have aliases," Jack said as he wrote the name on a pad.

"He's wearing a wig. I know it. His body hair is blond, and he has this black wig. He may also be wearing contact lenses, I'm not sure. And there's something else . . ."

"What?" Jack asked.

"I think he knows Edward Fields. I just have that feeling. Lesser offered to help Fields with his bags, which I thought was weird. Then they were sitting together at the wine-tasting table until I came in and broke it up. They skedaddled out of there so fast, I thought they were airborne."

"Regan, there has to be a computer at the winery."

"Yes. I saw one in the office."

"See if you can get the e-mail address. I'm going to get a copy of the picture of the guys with the tattoos and scan it to you.

Take a look and see if any of the four could be this guy Don"—
Jack took a deep breath—"which should be interesting."

"Okay, Jack, but we'll have to hurry. Don said he was leaving."

"The last thing I want to do is lose any one of this group."

"Let me go to the office, and I'll call you right back," Regan said.

Regan went out the door just as Don was coming down the hall.

"Hello, Don," she said.

"Hello, Regan," he answered.

Regan quickened her step. The way he said her name gave Regan the creeps.

Out by the reception desk, all was quiet. Regan knew her parents were resting, as was Lucretia, who had gone to her room to relax before cocktails. Regan found Lilac in the office.

"Regan, it's so wonderful having your parents here," Lilac began.

"Lilac," Regan said quickly. She knew she couldn't tell her specifically what it was about—not yet, anyway. "My friend Jack, whom you met the other day, is in New York and needs to send a picture to me. It has to do with a case he's working on. Could I possibly have him send the picture to me on your computer?"

"Oh, sure, Regan." Lilac wrote down her e-mail address and clicked on the computer to her e-mail box. "Call Jack and tell him to send it now. You'll know when it arrives. I'll get out of your way." Lilac got up and started to walk out of the room. "I've got so much to do to get ready for tonight anyway! It's going to be such fun. I'll be in the kitchen. If you don't mind, let me know if anyone rings the bell at the front desk."

"Absolutely," Regan promised. She was already dialing Jack's number.

"Jack, I'm in the office at the computer. Here's the e-mail address . . ."

"Great. Hold on." He handed the address to an assistant. "Scan the picture," he told him brusquely. "Hurry."

Regan felt as though her body was in a high state of alert. Her heart was pounding. So much for this morning's relaxation class. She and Jack hadn't even talked about how they'd handle it if she thought Don Lesser was one of the suspects in the picture.

"Regan," Jack said as he returned to the phone. "I have another call I've got to take. Let me call you right back on your cell phone."

"Okay." Regan sat staring at the computer. A moment later a new e-mail appeared. It was from Jack. She clicked on the message and watched as bit by bit the picture began to take shape on the screen. Adrenaline shot through her body as the photo became clearer. The guy on the left. He had blond hair, but his features, build, and smile were those of Don Lesser. Not that she'd seen him smile much. Regan stared closely at the photo. The taut stomach with the blond hair was definitely the same midriff she'd seen this morning.

There was no doubt it was Don Lesser!

"Oh my God," she said aloud.

"Helloooo," a voice called. "Anyone around?" Don Lesser came around the corner and into the room. He stopped dead in his tracks when he saw the image on the computer screen. The photo was in living color and big enough for anyone to see from several feet away.

Regan quickly pressed the delete button and turned to him. She could tell he knew that she knew. The fury on his face was unmistakable. "What are you doing?" he spat at her. He shut the door and locked it, then lunged at her, his arms outstretched and his fingers clenched, aiming for her throat. Regan screamed wildly, searching for a way to defend herself. She spotted a ceramic paperweight on the desk, picked it up, and flung it at his head. It grazed his forehead. For a moment he staggered back, but then he shook his head and lunged at her again. She kept screaming as she lifted up her right leg and managed to gave him a solid kick just below his tattoo. But he was like an ox. Her cell phone started ringing as Don's fingers wrapped around her throat.

His iron grip tightened, choking her. With all her strength Regan reached up her arms, pulled off his wig, and poked him in the eyes with her index fingers. Momentarily stunned, he let go of her. She gave him a second good swift kick and shrieked, *"Help me! Help!"* This time the sound was bloodcurdling.

Running feet in the hallway were followed by pounding on the door. "Regan! Regan!" It was Luke shouting.

Lesser spun around and released his grip on Regan. Realizing he was trapped, he rushed to the window, pushed it open, climbed out, and began to run through the vineyards.

The cell phone was ringing insistently. Luke was shouting and pounding on the door. Regan grabbed the phone and answered it as she walked somewhat unsteadily to let her father in the room. "I ID'ed the picture," she said to Jack. "He's definitely your guy."

59

Rex ran as fast as he could through the vineyards. What am I going to do? he thought wildly. Where can I go? He cursed himself for ever getting that stupid tattoo. It was all Jimmy's idea. They'd pulled off a big job, gone out drinking to celebrate, and the next thing he knew they were all tattooed. I should have killed Regan Reilly, he thought. I should have finished the job. That's what Jimmy would have done.

Who was sending her that picture?

Forget it, he told himself. Just get out of here. Keep running.

I know how I can get out of here. I'll drive Whitney's car out of the barn. It's my only chance. He raced down through the rows of trees. When he got to the end and turned right, the barn was in sight. He stopped dead in his tracks. An old car was parked directly in front of the door. There'd be no way he could get the Jeep out. Whose car was it? Why was it parked out here?

Rex looked around quickly. There was no one in sight. He ran over to the car, a tan four-door clunker. To his relief the keys were in the ignition. He jumped in and turned the key. The engine whined and coughed and died. Rex pumped the gas furiously and tried again. Finally, on his third exasperated attempt, the engine turned over. He put the car in reverse just as a portly guy came running from around the side of the barn with a shovel in his hand. "Hey!" he yelled.

Rex cursed as he floored the accelerator. The car screeched backward. He jammed on the brake and shifted into drive. He did a tight U-turn and took off down the dirt road, spraying dust into his pursuer's face. In the rearview mirror Rex could see his latest victim giving up the chase and shaking his fist.

"Go back to your digging!" Rex growled. He sped along the dirt road that at least was not as bumpy as the other access road to Altered States. Rex glanced at the dashboard. It looked as if it was from the sixties. Very basic. There weren't too many bells and whistles to figure out. And what was really easy to see was the big red needle pointing angrily at the big red E. Empty. Go to the gas station, stupid, it seemed to say. As he was approaching the main road, Rex slammed the steering wheel with his fist. Angrily, he made a wide right turn just as a van in the opposite lane was slowing up, as though the driver were looking for a turnoff.

Unable to avoid the inevitable, Rex hit the van's front left bumper, then scraped its side, which said GOS NEWS. KEEP WATCHING. The impact was too much for the vintage vehicle Rex had stolen. The car spun around and ended up facing in the wrong direction. The engine died. Frantically, Rex tried to start the car again, but it was no use. He was out of gas. He fumbled for the door handle and then jumped out of the car and started to run back down the dirt road just as a police car, its sirens blazing, came racing down the highway. The police car followed Rex down the dirt road and came to a quick halt a few feet behind him. Two cops jumped out.

"*Stop!* Put your hands up," a voice shouted. "Now!"

Rex kept running but turned to take a quick glance behind him. Big mistake. Lilac's black cat was out for a stroll and ended up directly in his path. When Rex turned back, he saw the cat underfoot and tried to step to the side, but his feet stumbled and he tripped, ending up facedown in the dirt road.

It took about two seconds for the cops to cuff him.

Lynne B. Harrison was squealing with delight. She and her personal cameraman were recording every last second of the drama. Within minutes the story would be replayed across the nation's television screens. It was worth every dent and scrape on the van.

60

W alter was furious. He was also stunned and more than a little worried. Bella was going to kill him! He had left the keys in the car, and it had been stolen. He had screwed up royally. But who could have imagined that their old junk heap of a car would be stolen in the middle of nowhere like this? Who was that guy anyway? An escaped convict?

After his prized heap disappeared from view, Walter stood grimacing and muttering to himself. What do I do now? I've got to report it to the police. But they're going to want to know what I was doing here. Then they'll look around and find the big holes we've dug behind the barn. I'd better cover them up until this blows over, he reasoned. Bella is definitely going to kill me. She's spent every lunch hour this week searching for her grandfather's treasure, and now she'll have to start over. It's all so unfair.

I'd better hurry up, he thought. I'll put the dirt back where it belongs, then I'll head over to the candle shop and we can call the police.

With the shovel still in his hand, Walter walked around to the back of the barn. When he rounded the bend and was faced with the sight of a dozen holes and just as many piles of dirt, he wanted to cry.

"This is so stupid!" he growled, hurling the shovel in frustration. It soared through the air and landed in the hole farthest away from where he stood, its sharp edge scraping the wall of the crevice on its downward path. Bits of earth crumbled and broke loose. It was the first hole Bella had dug on Monday.

Walter stomped his foot and walked over to retrieve the shovel. As he reached down to grab the handle, something red caught his eye. The bright color was visible through the wall of dirt that the shovel had hit. Walter got down on his knees and brushed the dirt with his hands. More and more of the red became visible. Could it be the side of some sort of container or trunk? Oh my God, he wondered. Could this possibly be Bella's treasure?

Walter grabbed the shovel and, in a frenzy the likes of which he had never previously experienced, began to remove the soil from around the mysterious object. Dirt was flying everywhere. Please, oh, please, he thought, let this be Grandpa Ward's treasure! Let the stealing of my car be worth it!

"It is a trunk!" he cried ecstatically when more dirt had been cleared. "It's a trunk, it's a trunk, it's a trunk!!!!"

Although the trunk was still embedded in the earth, Walter was able to undo the latch so the top could be opened.

He paused. Please let this be something really good, he prayed. Please let there be something really valuable in here. Slowly, he lifted the lid.

The small trunk was filled with old wine bottles of various shapes, sizes, and colors. Walter picked up a green-glass, onion-shaped bottle and examined it. It was stamped with a coat of arms, the year 1698, and the word "London." "Oh my God," he breathed. "These are beautiful." He picked up another. It had a different coat of arms, the year 1707, and "Rome" inscribed on the bottle. There are a dozen bottles in here, Walter counted. This is a collector's dream!

Just last week in the pub Walter had been chatting with some tourists who were wine experts. They sat at the bar until closing, drinking beer. "Once in a while we need to have a lager," they had joked.

The tourists told Walter that a wine bottle from the seventeenth century had just been auctioned for over £10,000 in Edinburgh. They explained that in those days customers ordered their own wine bottles from a glass merchant, then sent them to a wine merchant to be filled. The auction house was amazed that the bottle fetched such a high price. They had expected maybe £300 or £400 pounds at the most.

"Eureka!" Walter cried. "We've hit the jackpot!" Quickly he looked around to make sure no one was lurking nearby, ready to steal Bella's—and his—treasure. They had already stolen his car, but he didn't care about that anymore. These bottles could potentially turn into several hundred thousand dollars in the bank! He and Bella could both buy new cars. Now there was only one problem. How could he get the bottles home?

Walter closed the trunk, fastened the latch, covered it with dirt, and marked the spot with several pebbles. Quickly he filled in all the other holes. After brushing himself off, he went over to the creek, rinsed his hands, and dried them on his pants, which only made the dust-covered chinos look dirtier. "I'll buy new pants," he laughed, and with a spring in his step, he headed to the candle shop. "I'll buy myself a couple of pairs of pants," he sang to himself. "And then I'll buy myself a new pair of shoes . . . and then I'll buy myself a . . ."

Anyone who spotted him sauntering through the vineyards would have thought he was auditioning for Broadway.

61

W hat is going on out there? Whitney wondered. Has someone come for me? She heard a car pull up and stop. A while later
she heard someone try to start it. Then she heard someone
yelling. It was all so crazy. Nobody ever came out to the barn. It
was at the farthest edge of the property and had been abandoned for years.

Utilizing some of her Uncle Earl's relaxation techniques,
Whitney tried to remain focused and calm. She tried not to
dwell on the fact that she was miserable. She tried to replace
her negative thoughts with positive ones. She even tried to
imagine that she was playing the part of someone who was kidnapped and about to be rescued.

Taking deep breaths was impossible with the gag in her
mouth, but she could still control her breath. Easy, even, she
told herself. Think pleasant thoughts. Slowly and methodically
Whitney wiggled her hands and feet, attempting to loosen the
binds. As she did so, she thought about Frank.

I wish I could just sleep for hours and hours, she thought. At
least it would be an escape. Then when I wake up, I might be
rescued. He can't leave me out here forever—or can he? Whitney closed her eyes and thought she could detect the vaguest
smell of smoke.

Please, God, let that be my overactive imagination, she implored. Please. But in her heart she knew it wasn't her mind playing tricks on her. It had been a dry spring, and the threat of wildfires was very real. There's no way I'll fall asleep now.

Whitney shut her eyes tight. Hey, universe, she pleaded, if you're listening, send out the message that I need help. Find me. Somebody, please, find me.

62

They just caught him!" Regan announced. She was standing at the reception desk and was talking on the phone to the local police chief. Red marks were visible around her neck. "He stole a car that ran out of gas on the main road. He sideswiped a television van from Los Angeles."

"I'd like to get my hands on him," Luke said vehemently.

Luke, Nora, and Lilac had come running when Regan screamed bloody murder. Lilac called the police, who were on their way to Altered States when they arrested Don Lesser. They had just phoned back to give Regan the news.

"His real name is Rex Jordan."

Lilac had run to tell Earl and Leon what had happened, and the three siblings rushed back to the main lodge. Now they were all standing around as Regan talked on the phone. Nora had her hand protectively on Regan's forearm, Luke was just inches away on the other side of her.

"Who owned the stolen car?" Regan asked.

The cop on the other end read the name off the registration: "Walter and Bella Hagan."

"Bella?" Regan repeated, surprised. "She works here at the winery. Lesser escaped and went running out the back through the vineyards. I wonder where the car was."

Lilac turned to Earl. "Go get Bella."

Earl nodded and hurried off.

"We're bringing Jordan down to the station," the chief told Regan.

"I'll call my friend Jack Reilly in New York," Regan said. "He's going to be very happy, and he'll obviously want to talk to you."

"I'm sure he will. Tell him to give me a call."

Regan hesitated. She didn't want to bring up her fears about Whitney—that this guy Rex might have something to do with the fact that Whitney hadn't been heard from all day. Not in front of Lilac. Regan finished the conversation, thanked the officer, and hung up. She would ask Jack to talk to the police chief about Whitney.

"I really think that now is the time for a glass of Weldon Estate's finest wine," Lilac proposed.

"It's five o'clock somewhere in the world," Luke joked. He put his arm around Regan. "Come on, honey. Sit down with us in the living room. We could all stand to relax."

"I will, Dad," Regan agreed. "But first I have to call Jack." She opened her cell phone and walked out to the deck. The late afternoon sun was casting a soft light over the vineyards. Was it really only two days ago that she and Jack had arrived here for a restful weekend? Regan dialed his number and stared out at the rolling hills. There was a faint smell of smoke in the air. The winds were blowing the smoke from the wildfires in the direction of the winery.

"Hello," Jack answered on the first ring.

"The things I do for you."

"What now?" Jack asked, laughing.

"He's in custody."

"What?"

"They've got Rex Jordan behind bars."

"I don't believe it!"

"He stole a car and had a fender bender. I told the police chief you'd be calling him. When you speak to him, would you tell him about the situation with Whitney? I know she's not officially missing, but I'm worried. I'm afraid this Rex has something to do with her silence. He was here when she left early this morning. Maybe the police can get him to talk."

"I will," Jack promised.

"And I still say he's connected to Lucretia's fiancé. If you could find anything at all . . ."

"I'm working on it."

"Thanks, Jack. Keep me posted."

"Regan, you're the one with all the exciting developments."

"Well, the most exciting development for me now would be to learn that Whitney is safe and sound."

"You and me both," Jack echoed.

63

Edward was a wreck. He had just finished talking to Rex—
who was planning to check out—and was heading back to his
room when he heard all the commotion. Edward looked outside
and saw Rex running through the vineyard. Things didn't look
good, not good at all. Would Rex rat on him if he got caught?

There was a knock at the door. "Yes," he said tentatively.

"It's me, darling."

"Come on in."

Lucretia entered the room. She had rested and primped and
changed into an apricot-colored silk pants suit. She was now
ready for the rehearsal dinner.

Edward, meanwhile, was in the fetal position on his bed.

"Are you all right?" Lucretia inquired with concern. She
walked over and sat next to him.

"I don't feel well," Edward admitted pitifully.

Lucretia put her hand on his forehead. "You don't have a
fever."

"My stomach hurts," he moaned.

"That's a shame," Lucretia cooed. "But, darling, you really
have to start feeling better. We have our rehearsal dinner, and
there's so much going on, so much excitement."

"What excitement?" he asked, feigning innocence.

"There was a man who attacked that nice girl Regan Reilly in the office. He's a fugitive, and she figured it out. But they caught him!"

"They did?"

"Isn't that wonderful? He's a horrible, horrible person, just dreadful. He's wanted in New York, and now they're going to get him. They say he's going to be behind bars for a very long time. Lilac just can't figure out what he was doing here. Well, I'm sure it'll all be sorted out before long. The creep." Lucretia patted Edward's cheek. "Everyone is gathering for a glass of wine now. Why don't you take a shower and see if that doesn't make you feel better? Then join us, darling. It's your night, too."

"I will."

When Lucretia shut the door behind her, Edward lay very still, staring at the ceiling. What are my options? he wondered. Would it be better if I told them now that Whitney is tied up in a building on the property? If Rex turns on me, it'd be better if I had tried to help Whitney. They might go a little bit easier on me. I can say that I only wanted Rex to detain her for the weekend, keep her busy till the wedding was over. I never intended for him to kidnap her.

But then it would be all over, he thought woefully. Lucretia would never marry him, and he might end up in jail. No. I'll take the chance. I'll ride this out. Whitney will be fine. She'll be released once we're married, and everything will be fine.

Edward got up, went into the bathroom, and got sick.

At least I wasn't lying about that, he thought.

64

Bella was in the gift shop when Earl came in, walked over to her cautiously, and took her hand. "I want you to remain calm."

"What happened?" Bella cried. "Did something happen to Walter?"

Earl shook his head softly.

"Then what?" she demanded, greatly relieved. Earl could be so irritating.

"Your car was stolen."

"Stolen? From where?"

"I don't know the exact location," Earl said. He explained what had happened in the office, how "Don" had gone running into the vineyard and then had stolen the car and gotten into an accident.

Bella's heart sank. He must have stolen the car from out by the old barn. But where was Walter?

"Go on into the house," Earl urged her. "I'll take care of things here."

Bella came from behind the counter and stepped outside into the parking lot just as Walter was emerging from the vineyards. He came running up to Bella, lifted her into the air, swung her around, and gave her a big kiss.

"Walter!" Bella exclaimed. "Are you okay?"

"Of course I'm okay."

"But the car was stolen."

"How do you know?"

"What do you mean, how do I know? It was stolen by someone who tried to kill a girl here at the winery. He smashed up the car out on the main street."

Walter was still smiling.

Bella started to get worried. "Walter, were you out in the sun too long?"

"Uh-uh."

"No?"

"No. I have something to tell you, Bella."

"What?"

"I found the treasure."

Bella jumped up and down, then whispered to him. "What is it?"

Quickly Walter explained what he had found. "But we're going to have to rent a car fast and go back for the bottles. I'm telling you, they're worth thousands and thousands of dollars."

"I can't believe it," Bella exclaimed. "Grandpa Ward collected old wine bottles. When he got to Canada, he hung on to newspapers and magazines." She lowered her voice again. "We've got to go in the house and call the police about our stolen car. What excuse are you going to give for being back there?"

"I was coming to visit you and took a wrong turn."

"But you dropped me off here this morning."

"I'm not very good with directions."

Bella laughed and gave him a quick kiss, and then together they walked into the main lodge of Altered States, looking as if they didn't have a care in the world.

65

Lynne B. Harrison broadcast a live segment from the scene of the accident. "Unbelievable!" she began. "We were on our way to catch up with Lucretia Standish at the Altered States Winery when we were hit by a stolen car! A fugitive from the law who had spent the previous night at the bed-and-breakfast at Altered States was the driver. We were right at the Altered States property line when the car came barreling out of a side road . . ."

They replayed the clip of Rex getting out of the car, running, and then tripping over the cat. The cameraman had hurried over and zoomed in on Rex's face.

" . . . The driver has been identified as Rex Jordan of New York City. We'll keep you posted on the details about Rex as they come in. Now we're off to meet up with bride-to-be Lucretia Standish. This is Lynne B. Harrison with GOS-TV. Back to you later!"

66

Regan stepped back inside the main lodge, glanced out the window, and caught a glimpse of Bella hugging a man in the parking lot. They looked exuberant. That's odd, she thought. Wasn't her car just stolen?

Regan accepted a glass of wine from Lilac and sat down on one of the couches just as Lucretia made her entrance into the room.

"Darlings," Lucretia said grandly. "It's time to celebrate."

"Will Edward be joining us?" Regan asked.

"I hope so. The poor dear has tummy problems."

I'll bet, Regan thought.

Luke and Nora were seated on a couch facing Regan. Lucretia sat down next to them. Lilac was pouring the wine.

"Leon had to finish a couple of things up in the winery," Lilac explained. "But he'll be along soon. Oh, look, here's Bella."

Bella and a man who Regan thought looked as if he'd been rolling around on the ground entered the lodge. Lilac introduced Nora and Luke to Bella and her husband. "And Regan, this is Walter, Bella's husband."

"I'm so sorry your car was stolen," Lilac continued. "Walter, where was it?"

Walter laughed. "I was coming over to pay a little visit to Bella, and I turned down the wrong road. I ended up at the old barn at the edge of your property. The mountains were so pretty that I figured I'd get out and take a little walk. When I went back, there was a guy pulling away in my car. So I came over here to call the police, and Bella tells me you already knew the guy's been in an accident." He waved his hand. "Can you believe it?"

Sounds implausible, Regan thought. And if my car were stolen, I wouldn't be chuckling. What's going on with these two? They both obviously like to play with dirt. Bella had disappeared into the vineyard during her lunch hour and returned with dirt under her nails. Walter's pants looked as if they could use a good soak in the washing machine.

"Well, call the police and have a glass of wine," Lilac urged them.

"Sounds good to us," Bella said. "But I have to get back to the shop."

"I'll tell Earl to close up. It's about that time anyway," Lilac said.

"If you insist," Bella agreed gaily.

Boy, she's in a good mood, too, Regan thought.

The door opened again, and a young man and woman entered the lodge tentatively.

"Can I help you?" Lilac asked.

The woman spotted Lucretia. "We're here to meet with Lucretia Standish."

Lucretia popped out of her seat. "Hello!"

"Lucretia, I'm Heidi Durst, and this is Frank Kipsman." She turned to Lilac. "Are you Whitney Weldon's mother?"

"Yes, I am."

"I could tell! You two look so much alike! It's so nice to meet you. Frank and I are the director and producer of the movie that your daughter is starring in. I spoke to Lucretia about playing a part in *Jinxed,* and she said to join her for a glass of wine today."

"You arrived at the right time!" Lilac noted, smiling. "Please sit down."

Regan thought the director looked uncomfortable. He caught Regan's eye, and she nodded at him. "Is Whitney here?" he asked Lilac.

"No. She's at a seminar today. We'll see her tomorrow at Lucretia's wedding."

He's not happy, Regan thought. I can tell he doesn't want to be here. Heidi, on the other hand, had no problem pushing her way in and taking a seat next to Lucretia. Frank was hanging back. Regan got up and walked over to him. "My name is Regan Reilly. I met Whitney last night here at the winery."

"You did?" he asked with surprise.

"You haven't by any chance talked to her today, have you?" Regan asked.

Again, Frank looked surprised. "No. Why do you ask?"

"I was just hoping you had spoken to her. We've tried to call Whitney a couple of times, and she hasn't called back."

This time the look on his face was one of serious concern. "Regan, I beeped her at about eight o'clock this morning. She always calls me right back. I haven't heard from her, either."

"Are you two involved?" Regan asked quietly.

"Yes."

At that moment Regan knew for sure that something had happened to Whitney Weldon.

67

Phyllis was about ready to call it a day. Charles had gone home
after several cups of tea with the realization that there wasn't
much either one of them could do to prevent Lucretia's wedding. If she wanted to marry this guy, then it was her
business. Neither one of them had any specific reason to tell
Lucretia why she shouldn't marry him, other than that they
didn't like the looks of him. Or the sound of him. Or the feel
of him.

"If you think of something we can do," Charles pleaded as he
walked out the door, "don't hesitate to call."

Phyllis figured that even if the wedding didn't happen, she
would still get the money from Lilac, because Lucretia was planning to give it to them anyway. It was like losing one round of a
game show but still winning the grand prize. Lucretia was at the
winery getting acquainted with her "family," because Phyllis
had called Lilac back. Otherwise that invitation never would
have come about. Lucretia would give the Weldons the money
no matter what. Heck, if Lucretia didn't get married, they stood
to inherit millions and millions more than they would have if
the wedding took place. They wouldn't try to cheat Phyllis out of
her commission now, would they?

Phyllis wiped the countertop in the kitchen one last time, looked around, and decided everything was in order. She'd be back at the crack of dawn tomorrow to prepare for the festivities. Right now I'll go home, put up my feet, and watch television, she thought. She locked the back door and started walking out of the kitchen as the phone rang.

She almost let the machine pick it up.

"Oh, what's one more obnoxious call?" she asked herself as she picked up the phone. "Standish residence."

"Hello, is this Phyllis the maid?" the woman caller asked. She sounded like a busybody.

"Speaking," Phyllis said.

"Oh, good. I need to talk to you about Lucretia Standish. I've been following her story for the past couple of days now on GOS News, and the segment I saw a few minutes ago compelled me to call."

"Which segment was that?"

"About the man who was arrested up at the winery."

"A man was arrested at the winery!" Phyllis exclaimed. "I missed that segment."

"Like I was saying, it just aired. They caught some guy who's a fugitive. He'd been staying at the winery."

"Oh my."

"Oh my is right. I sat next to that guy on a flight from New York to Los Angeles yesterday."

"You did?"

"Can you believe it? I thought he was a little rude. He hogged the armrest and looked annoyed when I got up to go to the bathroom and had to squeeze past him. Then at the baggage claim area he pushed his way in front of everyone to get his bag. We were both walking out at the same time, and I noticed that he was picked up by a friend. I heard him say "Hi, Eddie," when the car pulled up. What I'm getting to is that I am positive the guy who picked him up is the guy Lucretia Standish is marrying."

Phyllis digested this information for a moment. She wished she had seen the segment. "Edward picked him up at the airport?"

"Eddie, Edward, call him what you want, he and this guy know each other. I felt I should let Miss Standish know. She has all that money, and this fellow she's marrying doesn't seem to have honorable intentions. My sister married a fellow nobody could stand, but everybody was afraid to say something. He put her through misery, and of course they got divorced. Now all she can say is how come no one warned her. I hear this from her so often that I figured even though I don't know Lucretia Standish, I should speak now or forever hold my peace. If I can spare just one person—"

"Right," Phyllis interrupted. "You're sure it was Edward Fields who picked this guy up at the airport?"

"Yes, positive. When I saw him on the TV yesterday, he was wearing the same shirt he had on at the airport. It was pink. I noticed that because I just bought a pink shirt for my husband. Anyway, I saw you on TV this morning, and I thought you'd be the person to call. My question is, why is Lucretia Standish's fiancé associating with a fugitive?"

"That's the sixty-four-thousand-dollar question."

"I guess it is."

"Well, thank you for calling Miss—?"

"Green. Sherry Green."

"Maybe I'd better get your number," Phyllis suggested.

"Sure."

Phyllis wrote the number down and then hung up. She picked up the phone again immediately and dialed Charles. When he answered, she related the conversation to him.

"We must let Lucretia know about this," Charles said with intensity. "We can't wait until tomorrow."

"It's a tough thing to tell her over the phone."

"Let's drive to the winery now."

"Now?"

"Sure. What have we got to lose? This is important."

"Let's stop at my house first," Phyllis said, "so I can get out of this maid's uniform."

"Whatever you say," Charles agreed. He hung up and smiled. "Finally!" he cried, and clapped his hands. "We're going to get that little worm before it's too late!"

68

"ere's my television reporter!" Lucretia cried. She sprang up from her seat like a spring uncoiling.

Lynne B. Harrison walked in the door, followed by a cameraman. "Hello," she said, giving a quick wave to the roomful of people. "I guess you could say we hit some turbulence on the road to Altered States."

"I want you to meet everyone," Lucretia exclaimed. She started the introductions with Heidi, who had practically been sitting in Lucretia's lap. "This is Heidi. She's producing a movie that my niece Whitney Weldon is starring in . . ."

"Whitney Weldon is your niece?" Lynne asked. "I just heard her being talked about on the radio."

Regan moved closer to Lynne. "What did they say?"

"Well," Lynne answered, "they said how funny she was in the movie."

"Who would have said that?" Heidi asked. "I mean, who would know that?"

"It was a production assistant on your film. He was a guest on the show. He was on with a guy who taught some sort of acting seminar today, but they had to evacuate because of the wildfires."

"Whitney was going to that seminar," Regan said quickly.

Lynne looked at her. "She didn't make it."

"She didn't make it?" Lilac said incredulously.

The room was still for a moment.

Lynne stammered, "A-a-apparently not."

"Oh, no," Lilac moaned as the reality of the situation began to hit her.

"Did they say anything else about Whitney?" Regan asked.

"No, they didn't. They were mostly talking about the fires."

"I want to phone the station and see if the seminar teacher is still there," Regan said decisively. "Maybe Whitney called him this morning to say she wasn't going to make it. Do you know the call letters?"

"The show was called *Dialogue with Dew.*" Lynne turned to her cameraman. "Scott, do you remember the call letters of the station?"

"No. I'll run out to the van and turn on the radio. It's still tuned to that station. I'll be right back."

Everyone in the room remained quiet. It was almost as if they were afraid to speak and had a collective pit-in-the-stomach feeling.

"Maybe she just decided to do something else today," Heidi proposed optimistically.

Frank stepped forward. "I called her this morning. She would have called me back if she could have. But she didn't."

Heidi looked at him and finally understood.

Lilac turned to Frank. "I thought something seemed different about Whitney last night. She said she wanted to really talk on Sunday," Lilac said softly.

The look Lilac and Frank gave each other was one of shared pain.

A moment later Scott was back. He handed Regan a piece of paper. "They gave out the phone number of the station for people to call in."

Regan quickly dialed the number on her cell phone. An operator answered, mumbled the call letters, and put Regan on hold.

"Come on," Regan muttered.

Finally the operator picked up again. "Can I help you?"

"Yes. I need to speak to a guest who was on your show this afternoon. He teaches the acting seminar—"

"That's Norman. Hold on."

Again, Regan waited, hoping against hope that Whitney had phoned to cancel. Maybe she decided to spend the day at the beach, to go with the flow. Maybe there was a logical explanation . . .

"Hello, this is Norman Broda."

Regan introduced herself. "I'm with Whitney Weldon's family, and we're concerned about her. We understand that she didn't attend your seminar today. Did she call you?"

Norman sighed. "No. I was very surprised because she just signed up for the class yesterday. She sounded so enthused."

Regan shook her head. "If you hear anything from her, please let us know."

"My girlfriend is the disc jockey here. I'll ask her to make an announcement on the air asking people to be on the lookout for Whitney, and if Whitney is listening, to please call."

"Thank you." Regan gave him the number of Altered States and hung up. She turned to the group, all of whom were watching her intently. "I'm going to call the police. But since Whitney has only been gone since this morning, she's not officially considered missing yet . . ."

"But that criminal was staying here," Lynne interjected.

Lilac looked as if someone had struck her.

"I know," Regan said. "But we have to start looking for Whitney ourselves. She could be anywhere between here and the site of the seminar—which is about seventy miles away. I don't think she got very far, though. She was planning to leave here at six o'clock this morning. If Rex Jordan was involved with her disappearance, he must have been back before eight because someone here would have seen him coming in after that. That means he wasn't gone very long, and he must have been on foot since Whitney's car is missing."

"I'll air a piece on Whitney right now," Lynne offered, "and tell people to be on the lookout for her. Do you have a picture?"

"In the office," Lilac answered as she went running out of the room.

Edward appeared from the hallway and stood at the edge of the group.

"Darling," Lucretia said, "Whitney is missing."

"That's awful," he replied.

Regan continued. "If we all fan out—" Her cell phone rang. She looked at the caller ID, saw that it was Jack, and answered it quickly.

"Regan, I just got Rex Jordan's cell phone records. He has called one number repeatedly in the last few days. It could be our friend Edward's phone number. I dialed it, but no one is answering, just the electronic voice mail."

Regan glanced over at Edward, who had remained at the edge of the room, almost as if he was planning his escape. "What number is that?" she asked Jack. Regan repeated the number loudly and deliberately as she grabbed a pen and wrote it down: "310-555-1642."

"That's Edward's number!" Lucretia cried.

"Hold on a second, Jack. Is that your number?" Regan asked Edward, her eyes boring into his.

"Ah, yes, it is."

"Is there any particular reason why Rex Jordan would have called you several times over the last few days?"

"What?" Lucretia gasped.

"I . . . I . . . I," he stammered.

"You're an associate of that hoodlum," Lucretia screeched.

"I knew him in New York. . . . I tried to keep him out of trouble."

"You lied to me!" Lucretia spat. She took off her ring and threw it at him.

"Hugo or Edward, or whatever you call yourself," Regan said in a steely tone, "where's Whitney?"

Edward's face was as white as a ghost. "How would I know where Whitney is? I didn't do anything wrong. Lucretia, you have to listen to me."

"You do know," Regan continued in the same steely tone, "that if anything happens to Whitney Weldon, you'll be considered an accessory to murder. Maybe you don't realize that the penalty for kidnapping and murder in California is execution."

The sound of twenty-one motorcycles making their entrance to Altered States pierced the air.

Dirt came running into the lodge, followed by Big Shot. "The fires are coming over from the west side of the mountain. We just drove by your barn out back—it's on fire. Burning embers are flying around everywhere."

"We'll get out the hoses," Leon cried. "At least it's not the lodge. We've got nothing back there but a bunch of old machinery and junk."

"That's not true," Edward said in a trembling voice. He knew it was all over. "Whitney's back in the barn. She's tied up in her car."

Lucretia wailed as though she had been mortally wounded. "Whitney!" she cried longingly for the niece she had yet to meet, afraid now that she'd never get the chance.

69

Whitney knew it was futile. She was going to die, and there was nothing she could do about it. Smoke was filling the barn. The heat from the fire was becoming intense. All the meditation exercises in the world couldn't calm her now.

Why? she wondered. Why did this have to happen just when everything was going so well? She'd met Frank, and he was everything she'd been looking for. Tears started spilling from her eyes, dampening the blindfold. It had been such a short time, but he felt like her soul mate.

Whitney thought about her mother, who had raised her alone. I wish I hadn't given her such a hard time about naming me Freshness. She actually laughed. I guess it could have been worse. Mom said her other choice was Poetry. Yes, Mom was a hippie, but Whitney knew she couldn't have found a better mother anywhere. What Whitney was afraid of now was that her death would be so traumatic for her. Lilac didn't deserve that.

And Uncle Earl. What a character! He had taught her to meditate and focus. "You've got to pay attention!" he told her repeatedly when she complained that her mind flitted around so much. "Use ditzyness for your comedy, not in real life."

Uncle Leon used to roll his eyes when he heard that coming out of Earl's mouth. "Talk about the pot calling the kettle black," he'd say. Leon was the worrier of the group, the one who was behind the scenes and quietly made sure everyone was all right.

I'll miss you all, Whitney thought tearfully as she started to cough. I'll miss you all.

70

Drive me back to the barn," Regan yelled to Dirt.

"I'm going with you," Frank shouted.

The whole group sprang into action.

"I'll call the fire department," Nora said with urgency in her voice.

Leon ran out the door, shouting to the gang of bikers: "I need some help with the hoses."

Regan jumped on the back of Dirt's bike. He took off, driving around the back of the lodge and straight through the vineyards. Frank was right behind, riding with Big Shot.

Please, Regan prayed as she held on to Dirt's leather vest. Please let her be okay. The smell of smoke was stronger and stronger. They came to the end of the aisle of trees and turned right. The left side of the barn was ablaze in front of them. Dirt stopped the bike, and Regan jumped off. She ran over to the building. The barn door was on fire. She ran around looking for something to use to break down the door. Behind the barn Regan spotted two shovels on the ground. She grabbed them both and ran back around to the front. Frank pulled one of the shovels from her hands. They both pounded at the burning door with the shovels and managed to pull it open.

Smoke came billowing out. Regan, Frank, Dirt, and Big Shot all started shouting Whitney's name. The air was thick with smoke, and it was impossible to see.

"Whitney!"

"Whitney!"

"Freshness!" Frank yelled at the top of his lungs.

Inside the car, sweat was pouring down Whitney's face. She was losing consciousness. Was someone calling her, or was she imagining it? she wondered as she drifted off.

"Freshness!"

Someone was calling. Someone was trying to save her. She had to let them know where she was. She was so tired. It took a superhuman effort, but she mustered all her strength, lifted her legs, and started to thump on the back window of the Jeep.

"I hear something!" Regan shouted. "In this direction." Holding the shovel out in front of her, Regan blindly followed the sounds of the thumping noise. Then the shovel hit what sounded like glass. Regan put out her hand. It was a car door, on the passenger side. "I found the car," Regan yelled as she opened the door.

"Whitney?" Regan called, coughing.

A low grunting noise came from the back of the Jeep.

Regan reached over to the console. The key was in the car! "We're going to get you out of here, Whitney," Regan shouted as she climbed into the driver's seat and started the car. She held her hand down on the horn as she backed up and out of the flaming barn, not stopping until she was well clear of the burning building. The barn was now consumed with flames.

Regan had barely come to a halt when Frank opened the back of the Jeep. He jumped in, scooped Whitney in his arms, and pulled her out, resting her on the ground. Dirt hurried over and handed him his pocketknife. Frank carefully cut the ties on

Whitney's arms and feet, the gag on her mouth, and the blind-fold on her eyes. She looked up and couldn't believe she was looking into the eyes of the man she was in love with, eyes she never thought she would see again. "Something tells me I owe you a phone call," she said.

Frank smiled and brushed back a tear from his eye. "It's okay. Just don't let it happen again."

71

Bella and Walter were going nuts. They ran out to the barn along with Nora and Luke and Lilac and Earl. The bikers were helping Leon with the hoses. A couple of the motorcycle gang had stayed behind, standing guard over Edward until the police arrived. Edward was probably anxious for the cops to get there. Anything was better than listening to Lucretia yelling at him.

Huffing and puffing, Bella and Walter arrived at the barn just as Whitney was lifted out of the Jeep. What a rescue! Everyone went running over to Whitney. The firefighters came racing down the road and stopped in front of the barn. They scurried out of the truck, turned on the hoses, and got to work.

"Walter," Bella whispered. "What are we going to do about the treasure?"

Walter looked around. Everyone was distracted by Whitney. "I'm afraid to leave the trunk in the ground back there—it's made of wood. If these fires spread, the trunk will burn. Who knows what could happen to the bottles? Let's go get it. Nobody will see us. We can hide the trunk in the vineyards and come back for it tonight."

Together they slipped behind the barn. "Where are the shovels?" Bella demanded.

"They were right here when I walked away," Walter whined. "I don't know what could have happened to them."

"We both have two hands," Bella said. "Let's get to work."

They knelt down where Walter had left the stones, just feet from the burning building, and started to dig. "Hurry, Walter, hurry," Bella commanded.

"I'm hurrying," he insisted.

Like two frisky dogs they pawed their way through the dirt. The heat from the burning building was causing them to sweat.

"I'm glad Whitney's okay," Bella said as they toiled.

"Oh, me, too. Me, too."

They didn't notice Regan Reilly on the sidelines, watching them with an amused expression on her face.

"Here it is," Walter cried as the red of the trunk started to show through the dirt.

"Ohhhh!" Bella trilled.

They reached their hands down the sides of the trunk and heaved it out of the ground.

"Do you want to take a quick peek?" Walter asked Bella.

"Not now. Let's just get it out of here."

"I'd like to take a look," Regan called to them.

Bella whipped around and snapped at Regan. "This belonged to my grandpa, and now it's mine."

"We'll see about that," Regan said. "I'll get two of the bikers to carry that back to the house. We can talk to the Weldons about what they'd like to do with what was found buried on their property." I knew those two looked as if they'd been digging around in the dirt, Regan thought. But a buried treasure? Regan was dying to see what was in there.

72

Whitney was weak and coughing but insisted on walking back through the vineyards to the house. "I need freshness!" she laughed. She stretched her arms overhead. "I want to be out in the air with the people I love." She lowered her arms back around Frank on one side and Lilac on the other. They both supported her as she walked to the lodge. Leon and Earl were following close behind.

Heidi was trying to chat up Leon, whom she found very sexy. The way he had raced around directing the gang of motorcyclists and fought the flames until the fire department arrived got her all tingly.

Regan was walking with Nora and Luke. She pulled her cell phone out of her pocket to call Jack.

"More exciting news," she reported to him when he answered.

Dirt and Big Shot were carrying the red trunk back to the house. None of the Weldons even knew about it yet. All they cared about was Whitney.

Bella and Walter were bringing up the rear. Now it was Bella's turn to shake her fist. "I don't care what they say. Those bottles belonged to Grandpa Ward. They should stay in the family."

"I know, I know," Walter replied. "We'll see what we can do."

Lucretia came running out of the main lodge to meet her niece. "Whitney!" she cried.

"Lucretia!" The two women hugged.

"I'm so sorry!" Lucretia lamented.

"What are you sorry for?" Whitney asked.

"I'm so sorry that that pathetic excuse of a man I was about to marry plotted to keep you away from our wedding."

The police were leading Edward Fields out of the house in handcuffs. They stopped just feet from Whitney. She looked straight at him. "Why didn't you want me at your wedding?"

He didn't answer her.

"His name is Edward Fields, formerly known as Hugo Fields," Lucretia prodded.

"So," Whitney said, shaking her head. "What does he have against me?"

"Haven't you seen him before?" Lucretia asked.

Whitney squinted. "Maybe, but for the life of me I couldn't tell you where."

Edward looked horrified. "You don't remember me?" he howled.

"Sorry," Whitney said. "I'm not very good at remembering people's faces. Uncle Earl told me I have to focus more on that kind of thing."

Edward nearly collapsed. The whole point of keeping her away from the wedding was unnecessary? She didn't even recognize him? He wanted to die. "We were in acting class together!" he shouted at her. "We were working on a scene."

"Is that why you didn't want me at the wedding?" Whitney asked. "Were you a really bad actor or something?"

"Noooooo," Edward cried as the police led him to the patrol car. He began wailing. His thoughts were like Earl's wildest monkey, swinging from tree to tree. If only he had taken his chances. If only he hadn't contacted that idiot Rex. If only, if only, if only . . .

"Wow," Whitney commented. "He really doesn't like me now."

"Well, we do, honey," Lilac assured her daughter. "Let's get you inside the house. You need some food and drink."

"It's no longer a rehearsal dinner," Lucretia announced. "And I thank God for that!"

Regan pulled Lilac aside. "Bella and Walter unearthed a trunk behind the barn that her grandfather left behind over eighty years ago. It has some valuable old wine bottles in it. She thinks they should get to keep it. I have to tell you that those bottles are potentially worth a lot of money."

Lilac looked at Regan, remembering how she felt when Uncle Haskell's money went to Lucretia. She understood the feeling that something that had once been in the family should stay in the family.

"You know," Regan continued, "the shovels we used to break open the barn door wouldn't have been there if those two hadn't been digging out back."

"Say no more," Lilac whispered as she took in the sight of Whitney sitting with Frank on the couch and looking so happy. "I have everything I need. Tell them the bottles are theirs."

Regan turned to Bella and Walter, who were leaning against the wall, and gave them the thumbs-up sign. Bella started to cry as she rested her head on Walter's chest. "Mother will be so happy. Let's go call her."

"And tomorrow we go shopping for a new car."

◆　◆　◆

The Road's Scholars were busy preparing the grill and setting up the dinner in the backyard. In the living room a round of toasts was being made.

Frank and Whitney were cozy on the couch. Heidi and Leon were hitting it off. Nora and Luke were sitting side by side, next to Bella and Walter, whom Lilac had invited to stay for dinner.

Lynne B. Harrison and her cameraman were recording it all.

"To karma," Earl toasted. "What goes around comes around. We are so happy to have Whitney back and to have Lucretia in our life."

"And I am so happy to have you as my family and new friends," Lucretia gushed. "What good is having all that I have if I can't share it?"

They're getting the money, Regan thought.

"Maybe my love life didn't turn out so well this time around . . ."

They all laughed as Charles and Phyllis walked through the front door. Lucretia spotted them and waved. "But you never know what might happen," Lucretia continued. "Charles and Phyllis, come on in!"

"Phyllis?" Lilac asked.

"Yes, it's me. We were worried about Lucretia."

"But we just heard on the radio that that worry has been erased," Charles said as he took Lucretia's hand and squeezed it gently.

"He's in the slammer," Lucretia acknowledged.

"Well, I'd like to make a toast that they throw away the key," Charles suggested.

"Hear! Hear!" they all cried and drank heartily.

"This is so wonderful!" Lucretia exclaimed. "I don't know what could make this party better."

"How about us?"

Everyone turned toward the door.

Two elderly women and a white-haired man were standing in the entrance.

Lucretia looked at them, a puzzled expression on her face.

"Come on, Lukey!" Polly cried. "You said you'd never forget us!"

"Ahhhhh!" Lucretia screamed. "My two oldest friends in the world."

Polly and Sarah came forward for an embrace.

"Your two oldest friends who would never, ever, ever divulge our secret," Sarah said.

"Who cares anymore?" Lucretia asked. "I'm proud of the fact that we're ninety-six years old!"

"Lucretia!" Charles laughed. "You lied about your age!"

"What actor doesn't? And you know I am going to be acting again." She smiled at Heidi. "I have a part in the film Whitney is doing. I want to start a production company. We'll have so much fun, Charles. You must come out of retirement. We're back in the movie business."

"I'll drink to that."

Lilac raised her glass. "I have another toast to make. To Regan Reilly. If it hadn't been for Regan, well, I don't even want to think about it."

"Thank you, Lilac." Regan laughed. "I guess you could say it's been a busy day."

Dirt stuck his head in the window. "Soup's on."

Lilac pulled Phyllis aside. "I can't thank you enough for calling me."

Phyllis looked embarrassed. "I wasn't so honest . . ."

"Stop," Lilac insisted. "If you hadn't called, we wouldn't have gotten Regan Reilly to look for Whitney. That call saved my daughter's life. I can never repay you for that, but I certainly intend to try just as soon as Lucretia . . ."

Phyllis felt as if she had won the grand prize on her favorite game show. "The money's not important anymore," her voice quavered as she interrupted Lilac. "Knowing I had something to do with saving Whitney is what makes me feel like a winner."

Lilac grabbed her hand. "Let's go eat."

By the end of the evening everyone looked happy. They had eaten, drunk, sung songs, and had a grand old time. Lilac insisted that they all stay overnight. "There's plenty of room," she said. "I have a pullout couch in the office that's a Bernadette Castro special, and I have a cot I can get out of the basement, and . . ."

When Regan finally went to her room, she glanced out the window and smiled. The bikers were laying out their bedrolls under the stars. It's been quite a day, she thought as her head hit the pillow. Now it's only two more weeks until I see Jack.

Sunday, May 12

73

───────◆───────

Sunday morning was bright and clear. The birds were chattering and chirping, and the last fires had been extinguished long before dawn. Regan awoke and lay in bed for a few moments, listening to the sounds around her. It was nearly nine o'clock. I slept without moving once, she realized. Boy, was I dead.

She got up, showered, and went out to the dining room. Every chair was filled. The bikers took up several tables. Luke and Nora were sitting with Lucretia and Charles and Lucretia's old friends.

"Happy Mother's Day, Mom." Regan gave her mother a kiss on the cheek.

"Thanks, dear."

Lilac and Phyllis emerged from the kitchen carrying serving plates stacked with pancakes.

"Regan, could you go out to the deck and get a couple of chairs from there?" Lilac asked.

"Sure."

Regan walked out of the dining room, through the main room, and out onto the deck. There was only one chair on the deck, and Jack Reilly was sitting in it.

"I thought you'd never get up," he said, smiling.

"Jack!" Regan sat on his lap and hugged him. "What are you doing here?"

"I had a couple of days free. I thought that maybe we could pick up our vacation where we left off . . ."

"Not here! I want to get out of here."

Jack laughed. "I'm kidding. Somebody had to come and escort Rex back to New York, so I figured it should be me. I couldn't wait another two weeks to see you again."

Lucretia appeared in the doorway. "Darlings! Get moving. It was too late to cancel the caterer, so we're going down to my house in Beverly Hills for a wonderful party." She paused, smiled slyly, and winked. "Unless of course you two want to keep it as a wedding celebration."

"We need more time to plan," Jack answered. He turned to Regan. "Don't you think so?"

Regan smiled at him. "I do."

Sept. 2002

F   Clark, Carol
            Higgins.

            Jinxed.

                           32222800273676

$23.00

DATE			

BAKER & TAYLOR